The Casino Girl

The Casino Girl

Richard Haley

ROBERT HALE · LONDON

ISBN 978-0-7090-8842-4

Robert Hale Limited
Clerkenwell House
Clerkenwell Green
London EC1R 0HT

www.halebooks.com

2 4 6 8 10 9 7 5 3 1

For Bob Markham

Typeset in 11/18pt New Century Schoolbook
Printed in Great Britain by the MPG Books Group, Bodmin and King's Lynn

ONE

He braked his car on a roundabout and turned off the ignition. It wasn't a real roundabout, it was a simple two-lane affair in the middle of a tight complex of short roads, junctions, cul-de-sacs and a small square marked out tightly into parking spaces.

It was an area that had been designed for learner drivers to practise entering a roundabout in the correct lane, to learn how to do a three-point turn, to reverse round a corner without nudging the kerb, to park without concealing a guideline. The training area had been laid out for a driving school and had never caught on. The school had learnt the hard way that even timid learners preferred to be on the open road as soon as possible, learning the necessary skills in the thick of normal traffic.

The training area had been abandoned. The grass verges of its roads were now unkempt and overgrown, the lamps of its half-size traffic lights smashed by vandals, its sign-plates rusting or hanging off their boards, the road markings faded and indistinct. 'Must have seemed a good idea at the time,' the man in the four-wheel-drive muttered. The place had a sinister look in the fitful moonlight. It was like the outskirts of a little town from where, years ago, everyone had fled. The man supposed the land would eventually be bought by a speculative builder, though he could see it wasn't an attractive proposition, isolated as it was on the fringes of Bradford.

Another car now approached, a bronze-coloured Mercedes. The man in the four-wheel-drive thought: good, the bloke was on time. He was keen to get it over, to get away from this spooky place. The other driver approached slowly, often braking in the maze of short roads, but finally reaching the central roundabout, which he drove on to in the opposite direction to the other vehicle, so that when he stopped next to it the drivers' side windows were adjacent. Both drivers slid open their automatic windows. The man in the Mercedes looked surprised. He said, 'I thought it would be Danny or Trev ...'

They were the last words he ever spoke. A nine-mm automatic appeared suddenly in the other man's hand and shot him cleanly in the temple. The gunman sighed. That had been the easy bit. The real work was just beginning. He drove his car to the other side of the roundabout and got out. He *had* to have a drag. 'You're getting a bit long in the tooth for this class of caper, me lad,' he told himself.

He smoked half a cigarette, drawing smoke deeply into his lungs, felt a little less nervy, then carefully put it out. He'd never needed to take a drag in the old days. He went across to the Mercedes where the body was now skewed half-over on to the passenger seat. He put his hand through the open window and turned the key in the ignition just far enough to light up the dashboard display. He needed to know the level of the petrol tank. It was slightly over three-quarters full. He returned to his own car and opened the tailgate. Stored in the boot were twenty of the sealable containers that held exactly a gallon of petrol. Many motorists kept one in case they ran out of fuel short of a petrol station.

He made a number of trips to the Mercedes, thoroughly dousing the body with unleaded, together with the entire interior of the car itself. His instructions had been very precise: it had to look a thoroughly professional job, the sort of job intended to warn any others who might be tempted to pull the same stunt as the dead man looked to have done.

When he decided enough petrol had been poured he returned to his own car for the last time and began to assemble a Molotov cocktail: petrol in a bottle, a rag stuffed into the neck to serve as a wick. He lit the rag very carefully, then threw the bottle through the Mercedes's still open window. This ensured that he wasn't accidentally burnt when the gallons of petrol ignited. As the car flared in a ball of roaring flame he drove rapidly off, knowing the entire car would go up when the heat melted the fuel line to the petrol tank. Within seconds it had, the explosion lighting up the sky above the silent fields of the green belt. He wondered how long it would take anyone to spot the debris in such a quiet spot.

*

Crane steered his car on to the wide drive of the large modern house called Moor Rise. It must have cost a great deal of money. It had a garage big enough to hold three cars built on to one end with above it what looked to be a house-keeper's or 'granny' flat. The windows of the upper rooms of the main building were each elegantly gabled, the design balanced by the lengthy horizontal windows of the ground-floor rooms and an imposing front door with an ornate surround. There was a carefully tended lawn and borders planted out with spring flowers. The house was situated on the winding road that led up from Cross Flatts through open country to the high moorland.

The door was opened to him by a woman in a flowered smock. 'It's Frank Crane, ma'am, to see Mrs Todd.'

'She's expecting you, sir.'

She led him across a large hall and into a spacious reception room. A woman was standing in front of the window. She turned and came towards him. 'Hello, Mr Crane, I'm Helen Todd.' She held out a hand.

He took it. 'Hello, Mrs Todd.'

'Please sit down.' She waved him to an armchair and sat down on a sofa.

'May I say first of all, Mrs Todd, how very sorry I am about your husband's tragic death.'

'Thank you.' She nodded, dark-blue eyes giving a controlled but almost bottomless impression of sadness and pain. She was a woman of striking looks, with straight, dark hair, high cheekbones and full lips. She was probably in her mid to late forties, with a smooth, unlined complexion, and though her figure was thickening slightly it was still very attractive. She wore a coffee-coloured cashmere sweater and a long dark-brown skirt. 'I'm afraid it's not the sort of death it's easy to cope with. I suppose the death of a loved one never is, but had Humph died of a heart attack or some such it might have been a little more bearable.'

'It must have been a dreadful experience.'

'The police aren't holding out much hope. They're certain it's the sort of killing someone's actually paid to do.' She gave a grimace of revulsion.

'I'm not really sure I can help, Mrs Todd,' he said gently, 'not if the police can't get anywhere. They have the resources and the expertise.'

'According to Inspector Jones you used to be in the CID yourself.'

'Some time ago.'

'He speaks very highly of you. Talks in glowing terms of the work you did on something called the Reliance Security robbery.'

'I had luck.'

'I'll not be able to sleep properly, Mr Crane, until I have some idea who might have wanted Humph dead. I dislike that modern expression about finding closure but it really does apply in my case.'

The smudges beneath her eyes and the faint haggardness testified to that. He said, 'If it was what they call a contract killing the killer will be an expert in covering his tracks.'

'But not, perhaps, the people who set him on.'

She had a point, but Crane's old colleagues would have taken that into account too. If it was a gangland killing, and the Todd affair showed every sign of being exactly that, the police wouldn't be pulling out too many stops to nail a professional. They'd do a thorough routine job and that would be more or less that, considering that there were more deserving cases to call on their time and attention. Crane had been in the force and he knew how the force prioritized.

'*Did* Mr Todd have any enemies you knew about?'

'We own a gambling casino. We were doing well.'

She glanced round the big room with its many pieces of carefully polished reproduction furniture, as if to emphasize just how well they had been doing. 'But a lot of people wish they owned a casino. Some of them aren't very nice. I suppose it's the nature of the business.'

'Do you work at the casino yourself?'

'We ran it together. I managed the restaurant and Humph the floor.'

'You'd know a lot of your members personally?'

'I got to know all the regulars well.'

'Could any of them have had a grudge against Mr Todd?'

'Not that I know of.'

Crane had a slight impression she was speaking rather carefully. He wondered if that meant that for some reason she might be holding something back. He was silent for a few seconds. 'I have to be frank, Mrs Todd. I really don't know that I can help you.'

'Why come then?' The quiet tones couldn't conceal a

directness he'd found most people had who ran businesses and managed staff.

'You sounded upset on the phone. I thought it was the least I could do.'

'I'll pay whatever it takes.' Her heavy eyes seemed almost to be pleading. 'Humph, well, he just meant everything to me; we spent our entire working lives married and together. We slaved like dogs to get the finance to buy the casino. I couldn't live with myself if I didn't do everything in my power to get the people who did for my husband into a witness box.' The quiet voice had taken on an almost rasping note.

Crane didn't need the money. The Reliance case had yielded a substantial reward and he could afford to pick and choose these days. He had to admit the case intrigued him. Casinos had a dubious reputation but you didn't usually associate them with what was obviously the sort of killing that went with organized crime. It was a case that would make a nice change from the life-style checks, the inheritance searches, the bad debts and the endless divorce work for the wives of wealthy men. He felt the usual guilt that if he did accept the work his challenge would be her tragedy. But he always ensured that cases that looked to be as difficult as this came with a caveat. 'I might be landing you with a big bill and nothing to show for it.'

'If you feel unable to take it on I'll have to keep on looking for someone who will. It seems a pity, as Mr Jones considered you to be one of the best people he'd had on his team.'

He could have told her that without DI Jones's unstinting help since he'd had to leave the force he'd never have got as far as he had as a PI. 'Well, Mrs Todd, if you can live with the idea there's a good chance I'll get nowhere I'll take on the work.'

'I'm so pleased.' She gave a smile then that almost reached her sad eyes. 'Would you like a coffee? There'll be some ready.'

'Thank you.'

'Please call me Helen. I find first names help a lot.'

She went off and returned quickly with a tray on which stood a cafetière, cups and saucers. She put the tray on a table near the window and poured.

'Who runs the casino at present, Helen?'

'Me. At least, I'm there most of the time. Pete Dexter manages the floor. He was Humph's second in command. He's very capable and reliable. Knows the business as well as Humph did. Black or white?'

'Black please. Pete will have his hands full.'

She put his cup on a little side table near his chair and sighed. 'I worry that Pete might want to move on one day. I get the feeling he might be keen to run his own show in a bigger casino. It's that kind of business.'

'It would leave you in a very difficult position, I imagine.'

'Very. I really don't want to cross that bridge till I have to.' She gave him a forlorn glance. 'Humph used to deal with those sorts of things, of course.'

Crane drank some of the coffee and thought for a few seconds. 'I'm trying to decide on the best way to make a start. I think it might be best if I go to the casino and get a feel for the atmosphere.'

'I agree. Why not come as an ordinary member? You could have a meal, look round the floor, talk to Pete and Gerry. Gerry's Pete's assistant. None of the others needs know who you really are.'

'That would be best. I daresay Pete and Gerry will know a great deal about the members.'

'Eyes and ears of the establishment. They both spent a great deal of time being questioned by the police.'

That was going to be the problem, Crane knew, going yet again over such well-trodden ground. 'And you yourself can think of no one who might have such a grudge against Mr Todd that they could go to the extent of killing him?'

'I've thought of little else since Humph went, but I really can't come up with anyone, anyone at all, who might hold such a grievance.'

It was clear Humphrey Todd had rarely been out of her mind, but Crane couldn't quite rid himself of the impression she spoke with a hint of reservation. He said, 'I'll be at the casino tonight if that's convenient.'

'I'll look forward to seeing you there.'

'I need to spell out my costs, Helen.'

He'd guessed she'd want to wave aside any money talk but he was mistaken. She listened to his details of hourly rates and expenses very intently, even asking for clarification on several points. She couldn't check an instinctive pursing of the lips when he reached the bottom line, which was, admittedly, a possible hefty one. But that was what business people were like, especially the self-made ones; the habit of prudence ingrained and unaffected even by the mourning of a dead spouse.

Perhaps it was her work at the casino, her attention to the type of detail that kept her mind, however briefly, away from the great chasm Todd's death had left in her life. Because when he'd finished she said, 'All right, Frank, that all seems reasonable. You'll need an advance when such figures are involved, I daresay. Twenty-five per cent?'

'Helen,' he said gently, 'I don't need an advance from people I can trust.'

She gave him a smile then of sad but almost girlish warmth.

His doorbell sounded. Terry Jones stood outside.

'Terry! Thanks for calling. Come in. Drink?'

'I'd not say no to a small Scotch.'

Crane took him into the front room. 'Sit yourself down.'

Jones liked these all too brief visits to Crane's house. It was like walking back in time: the medallion wallpaper, the tea service in a display cabinet, the chocolate-boxy pictures, a telly with one of those great cathode ray affairs jutting out the back. He doubted they even *sold* them any more.

Crane had bought the family semi from his parents when they'd retired to the coast. He'd not changed so much as a teaspoon. He'd once told Jones he liked the impression of living in the past when he was at home. 'Before I'd picked up all the other bloody baggage.'

Jones was one of the few who knew what all the other bloody baggage was.

Crane put down the drinks. He said, 'I saw Helen Todd today. I gather you let my name slip.'

'She'd be wasting her time going to anyone else. She was determined to have a private man when it was becoming obvious we weren't getting anywhere. To be brutally honest, Frank, I reckon it'll be a waste of her money and your time anyway.'

'I told her more or less the same thing myself. She'd not have it. I'd be glad of any form, Terry, if there is any.'

'There isn't, that's the trouble. There wasn't enough left of the poor bugger to fill a matchbox, let alone an urn. Someone with the skills had done a very, very thorough job. He must have bunged a tanker-load of unleaded in the car. Had to have been a contract.'

'She says she couldn't think of any enemies he might have had.'

'That's what she told us. All right, gambling can attract some dodgy characters, but the casinos are very carefully monitored these days by the Gaming Board. I daresay a few scams go on, maybe even a spot of laundering, but I'm sure that's all it is, white-collar stuff, not blokes with guns and petrol cans.'

'It was definitely Todd's car?'

'One of the number plates was blown off when it went up.'

'And it was that weird learner-driver place up past the woods?'

'Weird going on spooky. It wasn't a bad idea but it just

didn't catch on. No one's been near it for years. A chap from the driving school says a local farmer might buy it but only if they strip out all that tarmac and return it to an open field.'

Crane nodded. 'The killer must have had something that seemed worth having to Todd to get him up there.'

'Agreed.' Jones sipped his Scotch. 'You can hardly see the bloody place from the main road. It was two days before the uniforms picked up on it. Mind you, Helen had reported him missing right away.'

'Todd had no form?'

'No. But running a casino he knew he'd better not have. The lad had been a grafter. Kicked off in a betting shop. When the owner retired he sold Todd the business, let him pay on the drip. Two or three years later he'd made enough to open a second betting shop. He had flair, he organized the shops so they'd take bets on anything: the gee-gees, the general election constituency results, snow on Christmas Day, the bank rate going up or down, any mortal thing. He also bought into the poker they do on the telly. He ran one shop, Helen the other. She had her head screwed on too.'

'Tell me about it.' Crane gave a wry smile. 'She might be grieving for Todd but it didn't affect her attention to the fine detail of my costs. But when Todd bought the casino, that must have needed serious money.'

'Not as much as you might think. The place wasn't doing well when they took it over. They improved the restaurant and took on the most dazzling totty in town as croupiers, installed a new lighting system. The lighting's crucial, apparently; it has to make the punters think they're James Bond and the totty look like Elle Macpherson.

'According to Pete Dexter, the under-manager bloke, really first-class cooking attracts a lot of people who may not even be gamblers, they just go for the food. So they have this great meal and then think: why not a stroll around the tables? The bloke gets tempted, tells the wife he'll just have a tenner on the even chances. The croupier flashes him the "Come on big boy, do join the gang", smile and as often as not he's hooked. Dexter didn't spell it out but I reckon they can be down a monkey on the Barclaycard by the time the wife's dragging them out by the lapels.'

Jones finished his drink, got up reluctantly. It was like old times chewing the fat about a case with Crane. He'd once been Crane's 'guvnor' and Crane had been one of the best coppers he'd ever known. He could never see him now without wishing he were back. 'Got to go, Frank. I'm on a three-line whip to take the wife out tonight.'

Crane grinned. 'It'll give you a break from working the clock round on trying to nail Todd's killer.'

Jones also grinned. 'No change down the station. We're going through the motions, but it's obviously a gangland job. So if Todd's got in bad with the big people and they've sent an expert to see him off, and we've not the slightest thing to go on, we'll not be wasting too many man-hours. We'll keep an open file for as long as it takes, of course.'

'Of course!'

'Sorry I can't be of more help, Frank. If anything comes

up I'll tip you the wink. How's Helen bearing up, by the way?'

'She's in control but she's hurting badly. She just can't rest until she knows who'd do something like that to her Humph. I feel sorry for her. I don't think I'd have taken it on otherwise, and I don't think I've got a realistic chance of getting anywhere anyway.'

Jones gave him a sympathetic nod and made for the door. That was Crane. His only real fault was that he'd never been able to stop himself getting emotionally involved. If it was a fault. A good copper needed to be strong on compassion however many cases of human suffering he'd handled, needed to enter the force genuinely keen to make society as safe as possible. And Crane had never stopped being that kind of copper, even though he'd had to leave the force some years ago.

When Jones had gone Crane made a phone call before setting off to the casino. It was to Jason, the man Crane and Maggie, his part-time PA, called the Man with no Surname. Jason was one of that obscure band of people who could dig things out: details of people's lives, their current addresses, their unlisted phone numbers, their creditworthiness. It was the sort of thing Crane had learnt to do for himself, but it took time and it was more cost-effective to pay Jason to do it, who spent his working life doing little else.

'It's Frank Crane, Jase.'

'Hi, guv, how're you doing?'

'I'm fine. It's a bloke called Humphrey Todd, Jase. Ran

The Fields casino in the Bradford area. Someone torched his Merc with him in it not long ago.'

'I read the reports.'

'Anything you could come up with on his accounts would help, or anything on any villains he might have known. A general picture.'

'Leave it with me. How much detail?'

'As much as you can lay hands on. Look, Jase, I know sod all about the gambling business. I'm talking the dark side. Is it possible to pull a fast one on the Revenue, for instance?'

'Not easy. The Revenue watch the casinos like a hawk, as you can imagine, as do the Gaming Board. The Revenue work on averages. If you were, say, a self-employed Bradford plumber they'd expect your takings to come inside certain parameters for that area. OK, casinos are different; you might have a millionaire in one night who drops a hundred grand and the next night a bunch of guys on a lads' night out who spend twenty pounds each. But however much moolah crosses the tables, in the end the casino's going to be the winner and the Revenue will know roughly the percentage it's going to win by.'

'I think I get you. Whatever the amounts involved the casino's *percentage* of gain should stay roughly the same?'

'That's how chance works, guv, the way games like roulette and blackjack are organized.'

'Could laundering be a possibility?'

'I reckon it goes on but you'd have to be very careful. You'd not be able to rob a bank and launder that through a casino too easily. I daresay if you used more than one casino you could make a fair wedge disappear.'

'All right, Jase, I'll bear it all in mind. I daresay I'll have learnt more about gambling by the time I've finished this case than I ever wanted to know.'

'And what a mug's game, guv. I say stick to Premium Bonds. You can't win pussy money but you sure as hell can't lose.'

T W O

The Fields casino stood at the classier end of Thornton Road, where the lengthy highway, which started in the city, now ran through open country. There was plenty of parking at the rear of what had once been an imposing private mansion. Inevitably, Crane guessed, it would originally have been owned by a wool merchant or a mill owner in the middle of the last century.

Crane walked across an elegant reception area. A strongly built young man sat behind a desk on which stood one of the modern slimline VDUs. The well-pressed dinner jacket he wore did nothing to conceal the fact that he almost certainly doubled as a bouncer.

'Good evening, sir,' he said politely.

'The name's Frank Crane. Could you let Mrs Todd know I'm here.'

'She's expecting you, sir.' He pressed the key on a small telephone console. 'Mr Crane's arrived, Mrs Todd.'

She appeared within seconds, dressed in business clothes of dark trousers, long-line jacket and ivory scoop-neck top,

delicately made up, straight, dark hair smooth and slightly glossy. 'Ah, Frank, nice to see you. I'll just sign you in as my guest.'

She did so in a leather-bound book, the young man slid across to her, then led him from reception into a small circular bar in which several couples sat at small tables over aperitifs. 'Can I get you a drink?'

'A G and T, thanks.'

'Would you mind bringing a G and T through to the dining room for this gentleman, Norman,' she said to the elderly man who stood behind the bar. 'Put it on my tab. This way, Frank.'

The bar led directly into the dining room. Helen took him to a small table at the far end. 'We'll be able to talk here,' she told him. 'I ate earlier and I'll be up and down attending to diners but I'll keep coming back to you.' She handed him a menu, its binder also in leather and said. 'I'll be back when you've decided.'

She was one busy woman. Her role seemed to be that of maître d' and head waiter, chatting up people in the bar, then taking their orders for dinner, which two attractive women in black dresses and white pinafores actually served. He could only admire the way she concealed her unhappiness behind the easy patter and the cheerful smiles she gave the diners as she showed them to their tables. It was a polished performance.

A great deal of careful attention had been paid to the dining room. Picture lights glowed on gold-framed Impressionist prints of the dreamier kind: Seurat, Renoir, Signac, Matisse.

Thick carpeting enhanced the room's air of quiet opulence, the cutlery gleamed, the glasses shone, the table linen was starched and spotless and the napkins given the fan shape that required time and effort. A pier table stood midway on each side of the room, covered in fresh flower arrangements.

'If I could take your order, Frank?' Helen seemed to appear from nowhere. 'And then I must be off again. I should be able to find a clear window in twenty minutes or so.' She jotted his details down rapidly on a little pad. 'Enjoy your meal.'

There'd been few meals he'd enjoyed more. It wasn't an elaborate menu but the *Coquille St Jacques* and the duckling he ordered had been cooked to a precise perfection with ingredients of a superior standard. Even the house wine, of which he had a single glass, was of excellent quality. And though it looked as if Helen would be putting his dinner also on her own tab, he'd seen that the prices of the dishes were relatively modest.

When he'd finished his meal and ordered coffee the waitress brought two cups. Then Helen reappeared. 'I'll join you in a coffee, Frank. I should have a clear fifteen minutes now that things are quietening.'

'The meal was perfect, Helen, never eaten better. Thank you.'

'We have a starred chef, Frank, and a sous-chef he trained himself. Humph thought I was going over the top, but I insisted. Only business fight we ever really had. I said the food and the ambience must be first class; it would pull in people who didn't come just for the gambling.'

And then, full of fine food and wine, were tempted to play the tables and go home down a monkey. Crane recalled Jones's words as Helen dealt with a softly spoken query from one of the waitresses.

Turning back to him, she went on. 'I also made sure all the restaurant prices were kept low. The men are pleased the meal cost less than expected and feel they can spend the balance at the tables. Well, it's paid off,' she said, with a smile of modest pride.

Crane could only admire her for her intuition, her nerve in taking a gamble of her own, her ability to grasp the way so many men's minds worked. 'You must have been a formidable combination,' he said, 'you and Humph.'

She nodded, the forlorn look briefly back that he'd seen earlier in the day. 'What does the future hold now, Frank?' she said in a low voice. 'I wish I knew.'

Then she gave her head a little shake and sipped her coffee, 'However, let me give you a little rundown about how we operate. Out on the floor we have a team of young women running the tables. They're known as croupier girls in our casino, even when they're pushing thirty.'

'No men?'

'Not politically correct, but the members *want* women. They like pretty faces, they believe certain girls bring them luck, all that nonsense. We let the girls keep their tips, that encourages them to be smiley and pleasant *all* the time, the members won't tip girls who look as if they're just doing a job. Then we have the inspectors. On quiet nights it's Pete and Gerry, with Humph in overall charge when he was here. On busy nights we can call on licensed part-timers.'

'Inspectors?'

'It sounds rather grand, doesn't it. What they do is move round the tables making sure the girls are operating the games correctly and not cheating or being cheated. They resolve any disputes, that sort of thing. But being a small casino we all tend to do a bit of everything. Gerry, for example, will cover for a croupier girl when she takes her break.' She smiled faintly. 'And if we have any real trouble, though that's very rare with the type of people we attract, there's Keith, the rather large young man you saw at the door. He's an amateur boxer and he just needs to come on the floor and stand there for people to become very, very quiet.'

'And that's more or less it as far as the floor goes?'

'More or less. Apart from relief staff and part-timers, Pete, Gerry and the girls are the core staff out there, with Pete in charge since Humph died, and he's run ragged, to be honest.'

'And so far no one knows you've set me on?'

'Do you want me to speak to Pete tonight?'

'I think it would be best if I stayed anonymous for the time being. I'd just like to spend a night or two soaking up the atmosphere.'

'Very well. I'll arrange for you to become a member, just in case I'm not around to sign you in. Keith will have the form ready when you leave. And now I must shoot off again. See you later.'

Access to the floor was through an opening at the rear of the bar area and down three steps. The gambling room was a lengthy parallelogram that would have called for the knocking through of several of the mansion's original rooms. There were a great many planters, carefully sited and tended, containing the sorts of plants that were unaffected by artificial light and whose broad leaves seemed almost polished, their blossoms rich and delicately scented. Terry Jones had told him the lighting was very important and Crane could see that a great deal of expertise had gone into it, with its dramatic contrasts of shade and the soft, even light that glowed over the tables, with a subtle key light to enhance the looks of the attractive croupier girls. The girls were uniformly dressed in long skirts, crisp white shirts, floppy bow ties and elegant dark-red waistcoats. Their hairstyles were immaculate.

Crane moved slowly round the tables, as did several other people, as if deciding which table to join. He was quickly clocked by one of the two young men who also moved round the room and given the standard wide smile and a 'Good evening, sir'. Both men wore evening clothes, though with waistcoats instead of jackets. There were six tables, but two at the top end of the room were not operating. There were two blackjack set-ups, one on each side of the room, their curved tables set near the wall, both in use. It was clear the croupier girls had kept Helen Todd's warnings in mind. They were all very smiley and pleasant while exchanging chips for cash, spinning wheels, paying out winners and raking in the counters of losers.

There were a good many well-dressed Asians among the gamblers, a fair number of the sorts of couples who'd eaten well and inexpensively and convinced themselves they'd not spend a penny more than twenty pounds at the tables, several young men in business suits who gave a slightly wild-eyed impression of longing to live dangerously after days of grinding boredom in offices. They were of a type, Crane guessed, who could easily end the evening losing a good deal more than their shirts. And then there were a number of older men and women who played calmly but for high stakes, carefully balancing the six-lines and the corners against the columns and the even chances. The men had gold watches and cuff links and the women wore designer clothes and expensive jewellery. They were all clearly well off and gave the impression of gambling to sensible budgets that they'd not exceed.

There was one man who didn't quite fit into any of the other categories. He was well-dressed in a navy chino jacket, blue cotton shirt and a silk cravat. He was strongly built though lean with carefully cut greying hair which he wore in a long style, and he had good-looking regular features which had a slight swarthiness that gave them a Mediterranean cast. He looked to be about fifty. He put down high-value chips in a number of combinations at each spin of the wheel and seemed impervious to winning or losing. He had neither the tenseness of people who were breaking into the mortgage money, the animation of people who'd convinced themselves they were having nothing more than a fun flutter, nor the composed and absorbed look of the wealthy types who simply loved gambling as a hobby.

The man smiled often at the croupier girl. Without neglecting the other gamblers she gave him a good deal of what was special attention, always paying out his winnings or raking in his losses first. 'Well done, Mr Romano!' she said quietly at one point, when he'd had a hefty win on a corner. The man beamed and tossed back to her one of the chips, making it clear why he was so well looked after.

Each time the croupier girl had politely advised that betting was ended, spun the wheel to set the little ball hopping and rattling along the red and black grooves, the man called Romano barely glanced at the wheel but would gaze about the long room, apparently taking in the planters and the skilled lighting and the richly papered walls. It was a curiously intent look, the sort of look someone might give the interior of a house they were considering buying.

Crane moved to the roulette table he'd earlier selected and bought thirty pounds worth of two-pound chips, two pounds being the table's minimum stake. He'd chosen this table because of the croupier girl. The little gold disc on her waistcoat told him her name was Emilia. She was just as smiley and pleasant as the other girls, but she didn't project quite their brash assurance. She seemed to have a softer edge. She was about five-four, slender and shapely, and had long, lustrous brown hair, green eyes and a small well-defined mouth. It was the eyes that had caught his attention. He'd spent a lot of time over the years meeting unhappy women and he had an impression that despite the ready smiles and the agreeable manner she was, like Helen Todd, putting on a front, and just as skilfully. But neither, it seemed, could quite keep a faint sadness out of the eyes. He was certain it went unnoticed by anyone but him, trained as he was in the business of noticing. What it boiled down to was that Emilia gave him the sort of tenuous vibes that meant she might possibly be helpful to him. When young women were unhappy there was usually a man involved, and if Emilia's bloke had cleared off there was a slender chance it might give Crane an in. In what way he couldn't yet tell. Perhaps through gossip she might possibly know things about Humphrey Todd that hadn't reached the ears of the police. Or Helen Todd's. All he could do was follow his instincts in a case as difficult as this was certain to be.

Crane began to play roulette with his modest mound of chips. He wasn't a gambler but he'd looked up the mode of play and memorized the options and the jargon. He now knew what straight-ups were and streets and six-lines and so on and what were the odds on each. He guessed that you could play for quite a long time if you bet modestly on columns and even chances. You didn't win much or lose much. He played for half an hour, breaking even a lot of the time but ending up eight pounds in front. It had given him a chance to study Emilia, to confirm to himself that there really was a hint of sadness beneath the obligatory impression of high spirits. He met her smile with warm smiles of his own when it came time to pay out or rake in.

With the money he'd won he put four pounds on a street

and four pounds on red as a hedge. It was his final bet. As life had a habit of reacting in his favour only when it didn't matter one way or the other, he won on both bets: forty–four pounds on the street and four on the colour. As Emilia paid him out with her standard bright smile their eyes met. 'You must have brought me luck, Emilia,' he said, tossing two of the two-pound counters to her as a tip.

'Thank you, sir. I hope we see you again.'

'You will, Emilia, that's a promise.' He gave her his warm smile again, eyes holding on to hers in a way that he knew meant only one thing to a fanciable woman, that you fancied her.

He left the casino and went to his car. He keyed on the radio to Classic FM and prepared to wait. He didn't know what time the casino closed, but supposed it stayed open as long as there were sufficient gamblers to make it viable. He doubted it would be any later than midnight as this was a weekday night, and in fact people began drifting out to their cars steadily from eleven onwards.

The croupier girls began leaving shortly after the last of the gamblers had gone. Emilia walked out of the reception area wearing a long brown wrap cardigan over her casino clothes and got into a small Citroën. From a distance he followed her car down the long Thornton Road. A few miles from the city she took a left and drove through Allerton and up into Heaton, where she drew to a halt in Highgate, parked at the kerb and entered a small terrace house.

He now knew where she lived. He drove to his own house which by chance wasn't too far from hers and went directly to bed, hoping he'd not be lying sleepless into the early hours, his mind endlessly revolving around a case he felt he had as much chance of solving as getting a straight–up on the tables.

He was back at The Fields the following night. Everything was much the same, except busier, the balls rattling along the wheels, the croupier girls working gamely on and flashing their welcoming smiles, the inspectors patrolling the tables, though he noticed one of the original pair was missing, replaced by a much older man.

Emilia wasn't operating a roulette table this evening but was behind one of the blackjack set-ups. He'd studied the rules for that game too and he drifted over to the curved table, where he joined a couple and two men. Emilia exchanged his three tens for chips and dealt him in on the next hand.

The house was running against them and even if they stood at eighteens or nineteens the house was tending to better them. There were hands the house didn't win, but it won too often to make for interesting playing and their indifferent luck put off the others, leaving Crane alone at the table.

'You wish to continue, sir?'

'Why not?'

'Let's hope your luck improves.'

He smiled. 'I'd think it had been much improved if you'd let me take you for a drink on your night off.'

'I have to ignore that remark, sir. I'm simply here to deal blackjack. You wish me to deal?'

She handled it very politely but he knew he was well out of order. He just wanted to drive home the idea of how much he fancied her. 'How about a nice dinner then? I know some good places.'

'Do you wish me to *deal*, sir? I'm afraid if you make any more familiar remarks I shall have to send for the manager.'

'I'm very sorry. I really didn't mean to break the rules. It's just that I was bowled over by your attractiveness. Please forgive me. Yes, go ahead and deal.'

She blushed but flicked out the opening cards. He knew she wasn't really offended. Women being complimented on their looks rarely were, unless the man doing the complimenting totally put them off. Crane was a man of unremarkable looks but knew there was something about him that women tended to take to. He'd worked very hard on his engaging smile and his sympathetic manner and he was now convinced Emilia was in need of sympathy.

He played three more hands and though he won two of them they didn't make up for the hands he'd lost. Even so, when she paid him on the second win he slipped two of the coloured discs to her as he'd done the night before.

'Thank you, sir,' she said coolly. She knew perfectly well he was a net loser and she knew why he was tipping her. He gave her a final warm smile, eyes steadily on hers, and said, 'Well, goodnight, Emilia, I look forward to seeing you again and I'll try very hard not to make any familiar remarks.'

He walked off towards the bar area. Halfway across the room he glanced back at her, standing beneath her key light. She looked quickly away but he knew her eyes had been following him.

The bar was deserted, members now either still dining or out on the floor. The tireless Helen stood at the bar, wearing elegant gold-rimmed glasses and poring over a sheet of figures.

'Ah, Frank, I caught a glimpse of you earlier but we're having rather a busy night.'

'I was hoping to have a word with Pete and Gerry but one of them seems to be missing.'

'Gerry's night off. I could put you in touch with Pete for a while if you like.'

'No, I'd prefer to speak to them both separately but on the same night. They'll both be in tomorrow?'

She nodded. 'I'll get Bert in again to cover. He's one of the stand-ins. Been in the gambling business all his life. Care for a drink?'

'Thanks. A G and T.'

She held a glass to an optic. Crane said, 'Helen, when I was in last night there was a man who wore a navy jacket and a cravat. Seemed very wealthy, gambled with high-value chips.'

She'd been about to add ice to his glass but her hand shook so that she dropped ice cubes from the tongs. She threw the cubes into a sink below the bar and dabbed the bar with a tissue. Then she added ice and lemon to his drink more calmly. But he'd handed her some kind of a shock. 'I … I think that would have been Alphonse Romano. He's an old friend of Humph's and mine. He owns a casino outside

Scarborough and several night clubs too; on the coast, I believe.'

'He comes over as a man of great charm.'

'Oh … he's a very nice man. The girls love it when he picks their table. So generous.'

He could sense her uneasiness. The slight hesitation, the hand that still trembled a little.

'What brings him to The Fields?' he said casually.

'Oh …' She shrugged. 'Moral support, I suppose. He's been very kind to us all since Humph was killed. But he's … well, he's a very go-ahead businessman and Pete thinks he may be interested in buying another casino. Bradford has two down in the city itself, as you probably know. He could be wanting to make a bid for one of those.'

'Or even The Fields perhaps?'

'He's said nothing to me or the boys. But I think he knows it's not for sale.'

But Crane thought of how Romano had looked round the gambling room so intently while the roulette wheel was spinning, noting, it seemed, every detail of the room's ambience. And he wondered why his mention of Alphonse Romano had made her so nervous.

THREE

Crane guessed that Emilia wouldn't be too early a riser, working late at the casino. He parked in view of the house he'd seen her enter on the night before last. She left the house about ten, dressed in jeans, a violet turtle-neck and a brown gilet. She walked down Highgate and into one of the small block of shops. She came out after a short time with a plastic container of milk and a loaf. He smiled faintly; it looked as though, like him, she shopped only when things ran out.

He got out of his car and strolled in the direction of the shops. She seemed very occupied with her thoughts and didn't register his presence as they were about to pass.

'Why, Emilia, hello!'

She glanced at him vaguely, as if her mind had had to travel a long way. Then she recognized him and flushed, her green eyes suddenly sharp with irritation.

'Are you following me? Or should I say stalking?'

'Absolutely not. I'm on my way to our Asian friend's for a paper.'

'And you come all this way to go to this particular shop which is only yards from my house?'

'All what way? I live just round the corner, off Toller Lane.'

Her eyes were still hard with disbelief. He took out his driving licence photocard and showed it to her. 'My name, my address.'

She looked at it carefully then said reluctantly, 'All right, I believe you, just. Now if you don't mind, Mr Crane, I'd like to have my breakfast.' She began to move away, loaf under her arm, milk container clutched in hand.

'Well, now I've had this unexpected stroke of luck, meeting you well away from the casino, I don't suppose I could buy you that drink I mentioned?'

'You're right, you couldn't.'

'Your choice, the King's Arms, the Fox.'

'At ten a.m. in the morning!'

'I was thinking more in terms of lunchtime. We could have a bite of lunch too.'

She sighed. 'Look, Mr Crane—'

'The name's Frank.'

'Mr Crane, what makes you think I'm looking for male company?'

'You may not be looking for any but I don't think you've actually got any.'

She flushed. 'What makes you think that?'

'Let's just say that when I saw you at the casino I could detect a certain sadness beneath the big professional smiles.'

Her eyes widened. She watched him for several seconds in silence. 'You see too much.'

'Could be.'

'Well, how do you manage to see things no one else does, including the casino people?'

'I'm a private investigator. When you've read as many faces as I have, of people who are wanting to control their emotions, you don't often get it too wrong.'

'A private investigator!'

Her face now paled. 'What were you doing at The Fields?'

'A little gambling. Even PIs have a private life.'

She watched him in another silence. 'Well,' she said, 'you're right. I'm trying to get over the death of someone close and frankly I'm glad to get to the tables. The concentration helps get my mind off things.'

'I'm sorry. Believe me, Emilia, I know what it is to be unhappy.'

He did too and she looked as if she believed him. He felt genuinely sorry for her. No one who was as young and pretty as she was on a fine spring morning should be carrying around such a weight of sadness.

She nodded, eyes unfocused. 'Thank you. Well, I'd better go and have my tea and toast.'

'But you will let me buy you that drink?'

She finally smiled. 'You don't give in too easily, do you?'

'I have a feeling you'd not think much of men who did.'

'All right. The Fox at one. As long as you can live with the idea it's not going to be the start of anything that means much. And if you're married or similar, forget it.'

'No wife, no partner. I once thought I was going to get married but the lady changed her mind.'

And, whether Emilia believed it or not, that was the truth.

'Frank Crane.'

'Jason, guv.'

'Anything interesting, Jase?'

'Your Humphrey Todd. Looks to have run a pretty tight ship.'

'Go on.'

'He was doing very well. Him and his missus were trousering the thick end of half a million a year. He made one shrewd move buying The Fields. He got a better class of punter in a country atmosphere than the city operations. It pulls in wealthy folk from places like Leeds and Ilkley and Harrogate.'

'They also have a restaurant with a starred chef and, believe me, the food is first class.'

'Well, two thirds of the profit was going into a shares portfolio and he was making that pay big time.'

'The shares were in both names?'

'Initially, but a lot of the gains from the shares account went into off-shores just in his name.'

'Is that so? His wife strikes me as being one shrewd lady. I can't see her being too keen on that idea.'

'Maybe she never knew, guv. He seemed to have been one smart operator. If the stuff was just going abroad in his name it gave him flexibility in moving it around. But apart from the shares money, the dividends and so forth, there seemed to be a fair amount of other money hitting the NQAs.'

'NQAs?'

'No questions asked banks. I can't pin down where that loot was coming from.'

'Could that mean what I think it means?'

'It tends to mean drugs or laundering. I don't know how he was getting it through the bank on the UK side without someone wanting to know where it came from. I could get a line on it but it would take a lot more time. It might be best if we just accepted that Todd was building up a fair old wedge outside the country and some of it looked to be dodgy.'

Crane thought for a few seconds. 'I think you're probably right. We'll leave it at that. The bottom line seems to be that Todd was just a bit crooked and might have been doing drugs.'

'The high rollers are often partial to a line or two of the white stuff. If they are driving in to The Fields from a long way off they can't drink much but a gram of coke works wonders. I reckon it goes on discreetly in a fair number of the better casinos. I don't think Todd was being crooked so much as realistic.'

'OK, Jase, thanks a lot. It might give me something to work on. The killing looked to be very much a gangland affair and that could be where the drugs came in. How much do I owe you?'

'Four hours, guv, usual rate. Let me know when you can

call in and it'll be The Reservoir, early doors. A doll called
Lottie.'

Smiling faintly, Crane put down the phone. The Man with
no Surname didn't do cheques, it was always cash in a
brown envelope. And he never collected himself but always
sent along one of his many female friends, usually attractive if a bit on the rough side.

Emilia Brown poured some tea, put a slice of bread in the
toaster. She still wasn't quite sure if it had been purely an
accident, bumping into Frank Crane in Highgate. But she'd
seen him continue down to the general shop she'd just left
from her window then seen him return with a paper under
his arm. And his photocard *had* shown him as living in one
of the roads that ran from Toller Lane, which was only a
short distance away.

She sighed. She was lonely. She was wary of men, all
men, but he seemed a decent bloke and he certainly
seemed to have something of that quality of ... what was
it, empathy? Nothing in the way of looks but if men were
too good-looking they could often be far too delighted with
themselves. He had a really warm smile and that big
strong frame. He'd sounded so sincere about being sorry
for her loss. And with him being a PI, that really was
strange, as she'd once thought, because of her loss and the
police getting nowhere, that it might be worth contacting
a PI. But then she'd found out the truth for herself and
hadn't needed one. A single tear ran down the side of her
nose.

*

He was waiting in a corner of the busy bar-parlour. 'Hello again, Emilia. What can I get you?'

'A vodka and coke, please. And I tend to be known as Milly. Mum and Dad don't like it but no one asks them.'

'Milly it is. A V and C is on its way.'

When he returned he said, 'I'm so glad I could persuade you to join me.'

'Maybe I was intrigued by your being a PI. You're the first I've known. How do you get to be one?'

'A fair number of us are ex-coppers. We have the training and if we're lucky we have the contacts.'

'Why did you stop being a copper?'

His face became still for a second or two. 'Oh, it's a very long, very complicated story.'

And not a very happy one by the look of it, she thought. He drank some of his gin and tonic, smiled and said, 'How about you? How does a young woman like you get to run a roulette table?'

She shrugged. 'Sometimes I ask myself. I used to work for the Revenue and Customs. I was good with figures and worked on VAT returns and advising new companies how to go about completing them. I went to The Fields one night and found it interesting.'

'It must have meant a big change of life style.'

She nodded. She wore no make-up at all, probably to let her face breathe after being covered with the cosmetic mask that enhanced her attraction beneath the key lights of the tables. She still looked very attractive but in a way that was more to Crane's taste, almost like a dainty illusion of her working self. The absence of make-up seemed to emphasize a little the unhappiness she appeared to live with. She said, 'I applied to The Fields when there was a vacancy and they rather snapped me up. I find it easy to sort out the bets and keep the wheel going. The more it spins the more it wins, that's what Pete keeps drumming into us.' She sipped a little of her drink. 'I was quite happy with the hours too, I'm more of an evening person. The pay's pretty good and we get to keep our tips.'

'What does the future hold for a croupier girl?'

She shrugged again. 'I'd like the sort of job Pete's got. He's acting manager now with Humph being ... do you know about Mr Todd?'

'It was a big story, wasn't it? Car torched on that old driving school lay-out. It must have been a frightful shock for you all.'

'We're still trying to get over it,' she said, in a low voice. 'It seems so different now he's gone. He was so full of life, so cheerful, so good at chatting up the punters. The women thought he was Mr Wonderful. He attracted a lot of the kind of women who had high-flying jobs or ran their own businesses. They spent an awful lot at the tables just to have him fluttering round them in the bar or the restaurant.' She ended on an odd flat note.

'Can I get you another drink?'

'No, let me. Same again?' She got quickly to her feet and made to the bar. He grinned. Working girl who insisted on paying her corner so that he'd not get any ideas. He couldn't quite get his head round why a woman like Milly would want to work a roulette table. She'd surely have had a better future in the Revenue and Customs. And without her mask of make-up she seemed much more suited to a job with a firm career structure, where she'd have good pay and holidays, evenings and weekends free.

When she came back with the drinks she said, 'I've seen you twice at The Fields but not before. You don't really strike me as the gambling type.'

'What makes you say that?'

'You get a feel for punters. You don't seem to fit any of the usual categories.'

He thought of how he'd drifted round the tables himself on that first night, steadily pigeon-holing the different types: the fun couples, the compulsives, the wealthy folk who played carefully. He guessed that Milly, being the bright kid she was, would know which punter fitted into which slot the second they put down the counters. 'You're right,' he said, 'I haven't the remotest interest in gambling.'

She paused in pouring Coca-Cola into her new drink. Crane watched her for a few seconds. He felt he could safely make his next move. She was obviously intelligent and he guessed she could be trusted to be discreet. 'I'll put my cards on the table, Milly. I've not been up at The Fields to play the tables. I've been hired by Helen Todd to do a job. If I tell you what it is will you keep it to yourself?'

She watched him in silence, her face giving no clue as to what she was thinking. Then she nodded.

'She hired me to see if I can track down anyone who might have wanted to kill Mr Todd.'

Her eyes widened. 'But it's a police matter. They've spent such a lot of time at the casino.'

'They've hit a stone wall. It was a very professional type of killing and they couldn't get any forensic evidence from what was left of his car. They think it was some kind of a gangland job, as I do. Unless they can get a tip-off from a trusted source they'll have to put it in an open file.'

'Why are you telling me this? I thought PIs liked to work under cover.'

'We do, as far as possible. But this is going to be a very difficult case and I'm going to need all the help I can get.'

'What help do you think I can give you?'

'You're an insider. I had an idea you girls might just know something, anything, that hadn't been picked up by the police. My instincts told me that of the girls you were the one I'd be able to trust.'

'So you weren't just trying to pull me?'

He smiled. 'I needed to break the ice with you somehow.'

She smiled too, though it was a crooked smile. 'You did a pretty good job.'

'I'm sorry. I know it seems I'm wanting to use you. Well, I suppose I am, if you're willing. It doesn't mean to say I don't find you very attractive.'

'But using me takes priority.'

'It's in a good cause, Milly,' he said gently.

'I suppose it is. But I really don't know if I can tell you anything the police don't know.'

'How well did you know Humph?'

This threw her. She coloured slightly. 'No … no better than any of the others. He was friendly with all the staff. Tough when he needed to be.'

'Would you say he was a man who had affairs?'

'Not … not that I know of. He was good with women, but he only flattered them to encourage them to keep coming back. But … but what difference would it make if he *did* have affairs?'

'I'm trying to put together a profile of the man. Let's say he *was* having an affair, an affair with one of those wealthy women who play the tables. And let's say the woman's husband cottoned on. And what if he was so jealous he wanted Humph dead? It sounds extreme but it happens, you just have to read the papers. I simply thought that among you, you and the other girls, someone might have had an idea.'

'I'm afraid I don't spend too much time with the other girls,' she said, with a faint but decided coolness.

He could believe that, unfortunately, if she saw her future lying more with the chiefs than the Indians. Her unfocused eyes told him she was thinking hard. 'Someone who might know,' she went on, almost reluctantly, 'is Gerry Bishop. He's gay, he has a feel for the gossip. The girls have a lot of time for him. He's good at sorting out any problems they might have; he often acts as honest broker between them and the management. But he's also discreet. I gather that what you tell him stays with him.'

'That's worth knowing. I'll be speaking to Pete and Gerry

this evening. Apart from yourself, they'll be the only people who know who I really am at present.'

'I really don't think they'll be able to tell you anything they've not told the police. They were both interviewed at length.'

'The police work under great pressure on a lot of different cases. They haven't always the time to work out the right questions. Believe me, I know. He watched her in a short silence. 'You say you don't mix much with the other girls, but I'd be grateful for anything you could pick up, anything at all about Humph that might give me some sort of a lead. I'd make it worth your while.'

'I'd not want any kind of payment, Frank. I'll keep my ear to the ground. I'd like to know too who'd want to kill a man like Humph.'

'Thanks a lot, Milly. Let me get you a bite of lunch.'

She lived such a different life now from the one she'd had before at the HMRC. She knew she could never get used to it. Not that she had to now. She could easily get herself a decent office job in Leeds where she'd never have to work unsociable hours again. There was no point in hanging on at The Fields. She'd only stayed on to see if Humph's killer would be found. She didn't think it was going to happen, didn't think Frank Crane had any more chance than the police.

How well had she known Humph? That question had thrown her. She'd coloured a little; she wondered if he'd noticed. He didn't seem a bloke who missed too much. Well, maybe she could tell him one or two things about Humph but there was no point as they were nothing to do with his death.

She smiled the crooked smile of the pub. She was pretty, knew she was pretty. She *expected* blokes to try and get off with her. That was sort of her right. It hadn't done her self-esteem much good to know that Frank simply wanted her as a sidekick. Not that she was looking for a boyfriend, or needed one. Except that there was something about the big lug you couldn't help taking to. Even if he was a bit too quick on the awkward questions.

She sighed, gazing out over her little back garden from her kitchen window. The forsythias were a mass of yellow blossom, reminding her it was spring. Time for a new beginning. She made herself a cup of instant. What did it really matter now if the killer was found or not? They said it brought closure, but she doubted she'd ever find closure, the sadness would never go, even if it faded.

Crane drove about the city on routine work. She was pretty and she was bright. She must have come over as being in a different league from the other croupier girls, who were unlikely to have begun their working careers in the Civil Service. That could have been a turn-on for Todd.

The slight aura of dejection she carried round with her, the sudden blush when he'd asked her how well she'd known Todd. There were two women grieving for Todd, he was certain: Milly and Helen. Two women sharing the same pain.

FOUR

It was busier at The Fields that evening. It was almost the
weekend, when he knew it really would be humming. The
croupier girls were working steadily, the expert lighting
emphasizing the attraction of their shining caps of hair, their
enamelled features and gleaming eyes. If you had to go home
down a monkey, Crane supposed, it had to soften the blow a
little to have your chips whisked away by women who looked
the way they did.

As he'd driven up the long Thornton Road, from city
suburbs to open country, the sun had been setting on
another clear spring day, but on the floor of The Fields there
was only one changeless mix of light: the dramatic elegance
of the pools of shade contrasted with the soft even glow of
the table lamps and the sharper beams that picked out the
girls as they flicked balls on to slowly revolving wheels,
placed little glass dollies on winning numbers, paid chips
out and raked chips in. There were no clocks in the room
and no windows, no distractions of any kind to remind the
gamblers that any other world existed outside this long

room, a room into which you could walk with a hundred pounds in your pocket and leave with £1,000. Or the other way about, Crane thought, with a faint smile.

All the usual types were here tonight, only more of them: the fun couples, the compulsives, the relaxed wealthy types who played a long, careful game. He wondered if some of the bejewelled women would gradually drop off now that Todd was gone, seeing that he'd been one of the incentives for their coming. He walked into the bar area. Helen was ticking off names on a sheet attached to her clipboard and handing out menus with her usual welcoming smiles and easy chat. It was a remarkable effort of will when he thought of how she'd be in the early part of the day, sitting in one of her big rooms lost in loneliness and pain and waiting, like Milly, for the evening to begin to give her a few hours distraction.

'Hello, Frank,' she said, when she had a few minutes' break. 'This is what we call gearing-up night. By Friday we'll be like people in those comedy films that have been speeded up. A G and T, Norman, for Mr Crane, my tab.'

'Thanks a lot, Helen. Am I in order to speak to Pete and Gerry tonight?' he said quietly.

'No problem. I've fixed cover for when they're off the floor.'

'Helen, the night Humph went up to the learner-driver place, did he actually tell you where he was going or why?'

She shook her head, the sprightly mask she forced herself to wear for the diners lifting briefly on the sadness that never left her. 'I only wish he had. I'm sure I could have talked him out of going out, at *night*, to a strange place like that. I was having my night off. The police asked, of course.'

'Had he ever gone up there before?'

'Not to my knowledge but I can't be certain. When I'm finished in the restaurant I'm pretty bushed and I sometimes go home if we're quiet. But Humph, he liked to see things through, work on the night's figures and so forth. He often got home very late, so he could have gone up there at some other time.'

If he wasn't seeing Milly or another woman. He wondered if she really believed that all he did when he was staying out half the night was check the till.

When he'd finished his drink they went down the steps to the floor and past the busy tables to what she called the interview room. Pete and Gerry were steadily patrolling the aisles together with the older man called Bert in their waistcoated evening wear. They passed the table Milly was operating. She caught Crane's eye as she set the wheel revolving. He winked and she gave him one of her trained bright smiles that hid what he was now certain was an unhappiness she shared with Helen.

The interview room was a small office next to the cash-point at the top of the room. It contained just a desk and chair, a visitor's chair and a filing cabinet. It had a raised floor and there was a porthole type window in the wall that overlooked the gambling room. Crane was learning that every peripheral room had a window or opening that overlooked the floor. Helen had spoken a few quiet words to Pete during their progress and he came into the room shortly after them. He gave Crane a questioning glance. 'Pete,' Helen said, 'I daresay you'll know this gentleman by sight.'

'You've been in twice before, sir. You played a little roulette the first time and a little blackjack the second.'

Crane was impressed, Pete wasn't a man who missed too much. It could be very helpful. Helen said, 'His name's Frank Crane, Pete. He's a private investigator who used to be a police detective. He's agreed to work for me to see if he can turn up anything, anything at all, about who killed Humph. As you know, the police have got nowhere.'

'How do you do, Pete.' Crane held out a hand. Dexter took it with the wide friendly smile that all the staff could turn on like actors. 'Pleased to meet you, Frank. I don't know if there's anything I can tell you that I haven't told the police.'

'That's going to be the problem, I'm afraid. I'll be pleased if you just tell me what you told them.'

'I'll leave you chaps to it,' Helen said. 'I've got a party of eight coming in any time now. Pete will send Gerry in when you've finished.'

Crane gave Dexter one of the reassuring smiles that were part of his own stock-in-trade, 'I'm trying to get an outline of how the casino works, Pete. Give me a rundown of what you and Gerry actually do, if you wouldn't mind.'

'I'll not sit down, Frank. I need to keep an eye on what's going on out there. Story of my life.'

'That's OK, I'll stand too. This shouldn't take long. I'm impressed by that memory of yours.'

Dexter shrugged. 'Goes with the job.' Eyes flickering over the floor through the porthole window, he said, 'I was assistant manager to Mr Todd. I'm acting manager now, though Helen's the real boss. She can do anything we can do nearly as well as we can, plus running the restaurant.'

He was a man of middle height and strongly built, straight fair hair, neatly parted on the left, deep-set brown eyes that seemed as vigilant as a bird's, strong features that, when they weren't arranged in the house smile, were impassive, which Crane thought was probably a useful quality in a man supervising gambling tables.

'Helen did say you all knew how to multi-task,' Crane said.

Dexter nodded. 'We have to be prepared to tackle anything. This isn't Las Vegas or the Ritz where they have large staffs and people do just the one thing: inspector, pit-boss, manager, all that. When Humph was alive, him, Helen, Gerry and me were the basic team.'

'When you move round the tables what exactly are you looking out for?'

'We have to make sure the croupier girls don't make mistakes paying out, either accidentally or on purpose. We've had one or two girls in the past trying to work a scam with a boyfriend. We have to be sure members with big winnings have come by them honestly. And then there's card-counting on the blackjack tables.'

'Card-counting?'

'Half a dozen blokes come in the casino separately, as if they don't know each other. They drift towards a blackjack table. One of them has a trained memory, he can remember every card out of the shoe. This helps him to bet strategically, especially if too many picture cards come towards the end of the shoe. It's to do with the punter being able to stick at sixteen or lower but not the dealer. We have to knock all that on the head as it buggers up the house advantage of five or six per cent.' He gave a wry grin. 'It's supposed to be a fun gambling game. If the house has no advantage we might as well close down.'

'Does that go on much?'

He shook his head. 'We get a decent class of member on the whole. You get a nose for the docs.'

'Docs?'

'It's what Humph called the card-sharps. It was some American saying he'd picked up somewhere: "Never play cards with any man named Doc.".'

Crane grinned. 'What do you do with these people?'

'I stand behind them, just letting them know I wasn't born yesterday. It gets them uneasy and they clear off. I don't forget the faces and they don't get back in. But we have to go canny; it might be a bunch of young guys on a lads' night out who'd not know how to fix a game if you let them deal their own cards.'

'Any roulette try-ons?'

'People have a go now and then, especially if they've had a couple. Try to slide a chip from an even chance to a double street's a favourite. But we give the girls intensive training, they know the dodges.'

'What if there's a dispute between punter and croupier girl as to exactly where his chip should be? Who decides who's right?'

'The camera.' Dexter grinned this time. 'Our old friend CCTV. There's a concealed lens above each table. They're linked to screens in a special room. We can replay the moves immediately, it's like a photo-finish on the gee-gees. If the punter's pulled a fast one, brother, the red face. He gets banned on the spot and his photo taken, which is circulated to other casinos. I say "he" but it can be a she.'

'Well, many thanks for the info. I'd never realized the complexities of the operation.'

'Few people do. They're playing and we're working so we keep as low a profile as possible.'

Crane wondered if any of this was relevant, could give any clue to Todd's death. A revenge killing by a banned member seemed very much over the top, unless the member wasn't entirely right in the head. But if that was the case would he (or she) really have the nous to arrange such a clever killing? What he *had* learnt was that Dexter was one very skilled and driven casino executive who, Helen was pretty sure, would one day want to run his own show. Even as they'd talked his restless gaze had scarcely left the casino floor, even though Gerry and Bert seemed very much in control.

'Pete, who'd want to kill a respectable businessman like Humph? I know casinos tend to have a dubious reputation with a lot of the public and even the government itself seems to be getting cold feet about the big American-style one planned for Manchester, but The Fields looks to be a class act. I understand quite a few members come here simply for the food as it's so good. Surely Humph couldn't have been involved in some kind of a gangland vendetta. It was almost certainly a professional killing.'

'We've none of us any idea. He was one straight bloke, kept his accounts properly and paid his taxes. I daresay he cut a few corners, what businessman doesn't, but nothing to get the Revenue on his back.'

Neither the Revenue or his wife, Crane thought, seeing that he had money tucked away in off-shore NQAs in his own name.

'Did Humph have affairs?'

'If he did he kept it very quiet. He did have a way with the ladies. He had the looks and the blarney.'

'Come on, Pete, you must have had an idea he was having it away.'

Dexter looked briefly aside from his endless scrutiny of the floor, which to Crane's untrained eye seemed as calmly busy as a Morrison's check-out, and gave him a slightly sheepish glance. 'For Christ's sake, not a word to Helen, but I saw him not long ago in a corner of a restaurant off the old Keighley–Skipton road, with one of our big-spending lady punters.'

'What's her name?'

'Evelyn Cooper.'

'Did you tell the police?'

'They didn't ask and I didn't think it meant anything.'

'She could have had a jealous husband.'

'Who'd kill Humph?'

'These things happen. If he was wealthy and had contacts.'

'Frank, the guy was shot dead and half a petrol station poured in his Merc. Are you telling me an expert job like that was done because some bloke was pissed off with his missus going up on the moors to have leg-over and chips with Humph? Do me a favour.'

'I just have to keep an open mind to every possibility, however remote. Does Evelyn Cooper still come here?'

'She's here tonight. See the croupier girl with the blond hair taken back, just clearing the table. Just to her left there's a woman with high-lighted hair and a silky tan top. That's Evelyn Cooper.'

'Could you give me her address?'

Dexter went to the desk, tapped keys on a VDU. He read out the details of a Cullingworth address which Crane wrote in his notebook. Dexter knew as well as Crane that he was clutching at straws, but just occasionally Crane found he'd taken hold of a sheaf and not a straw.

'Thanks for this. Now this Alphonse Romano bloke ...'

He'd thrown in the name without warning to see if it got a reaction. It had certainly got one from Helen. Dexter's eyes abruptly stopped their ceaseless flickering over the floor, but he gave no other sign of having been given a start. But as Crane was beginning to find out, he was highly skilled in concealing his reactions. 'Alphonse Romano. He owns a casino near Scarborough and comes here once, maybe twice a week.'

'The first night I was here Romano was betting heavily with those high-value oblong chips.'

'Biscuits in the jargon. That would be one of the tables

with a high min and max. When Humph was alive we were trying to decide if we had enough high rollers to invest in a *salon privé*; that's an exclusive room just for the very wealthy punters. It would mean rearranging the dining room.'

Crane didn't need to know about biscuits or *salons privés*. He wondered why Dexter was waffling. He said, 'If Romano owns a Scarborough casino why does he spend so much time at The Fields?'

'He was a good friend of Humph's when he was alive. Humph and Helen in fact. Him and Humph, they'd swap gossip, warn each other about the docs, swap information on lay-out improvement and keeping costs down. Have you seen the ATM on the wall outside the cage? It replaced an assistant cashier. That was one of Mr Romano's tips.'

'But why does he keep coming to Bradford now that Humph's dead?'

'He's a sharp businessman. He may be wanting to buy another casino.'

'Like The Fields?'

'I think he knows it's not for sale.'

'Have you had dealings with Romano yourself?'

Once more those tireless deep-set eyes became still for a few seconds. 'Only when he and Humph were talking things over and Humph asked me to sit in. That's how I was advised to install an ATM.'

'How long have you been in this business, Pete?'

Dexter flashed him another of his birdlike glances. 'Right from leaving school. I started work with old Bert out there in a betting shop. He sold out to Humph and Humph brought me with him to The Fields.'

Crane nodded. He was getting nowhere. Dexter knew the gambling game backwards, knew what had really gone on at The Fields, more than he was ready to let on about. Humphrey Todd had been filtering money abroad. His car had been blown up in what looked almost certain to have been a gangland murder. Dexter must surely have had some idea what was really going on if, say, Todd really was involved in laundering and drugs. But Dexter was playing a straight bat, he was convinced of it: see nothing, hear nothing and say sod-all. Could it be that Todd had been bunging Dexter a backhander to *keep* his mouth shut? With a man who had as much self-control as Dexter he doubted he'd ever get to know anything he could really use.

'Well, thanks, Pete, you've been very helpful. Tell me, a man as skilled in casino work as you, do you not get head-hunted now and then?'

Dexter's briefly motionless eyes were saying it all as usual, not that Crane had any real clue as to what they were saying. 'I ... think they know in the business that I'm settled here. Humph once said not to take it as definite but he and Helen might pull out in a few years. He'd not sell up, but have a manager take over and run it on a profit-share basis. He asked would I be interested. I told him I'd snap his hand off. But then he goes and gets himself torched.'

There was no emotion in his tone, no traces of bitterness about the crappy hand fate had dealt him; he spoke in the same even way he'd spoken for the past fifteen minutes. Yet if Helen *did* eventually decide to sell up, though Dexter could probably be sure of his present job, he could kiss goodbye to any profit-share.

'I'm sorry about that, Pete. I hope things work out for you when the dust settles. I'll let you get back to the floor. Would you ask Gerry to step in?'

A few seconds later there was a tap at the door and Bishop came in. 'You wanted to see me, Mr Crane.'

'The name's Frank, Gerry.' He shook his hand. 'We can either sit or stand. Your colleague preferred to stand and keep an eye on the floor.'

'He would. Oh no, I'll sit, Frank. Take the weight off my feet. I keep telling Pete, we'll have varicose veins like bell-ropes, all the standing we get to do.'

It was clear Bishop lacked the intense dedication that had kept Dexter on guard at the porthole window.

'Gerry, do you know what I am?'

'A private detective, according to Pete. Trying to find out who did for Humph.'

'Pete's given me an excellent run-down of how you chaps operate, keeping an eye out for card-sharps and so forth.'

Bishop raised his hand in a fluttering gesture. 'Tell me about it. We had one in last month, never seen the likes. Beautifully turned out: worsted suit, silk tie, lovely cuff links, soft leather loafers, a haircut no barber in Bradford could have risen to. Well, wasn't he clocking every card out of the shoe? And there can be five or six decks; think on. He was using a system called Basic Strategy. I almost felt he deserved to beat the house if he could remember that lot. Oh dear, what am I *saying*.'

Crane smiled. 'But you nailed him?'

'Out through the door like a ferret up a drainpipe. Never saw him again.' There was a faint note of regret in his voice that hinted that he personally wouldn't at all have minded seeing him again.

'Gerry, Helen hired me just to see if I could turn up anything at all on who killed Humph. I've stressed to her that I don't think there's much chance, though of course I'll do my best.'

'She wants closure, doesn't she, poor thing.' A look of what seemed genuine sadness passed over Bishop's face. For a few seconds he looked almost forlorn. It made a striking contrast to Dexter's total absence of any emotion. Crane wondered if he'd been attached to Todd, as gay men sometimes were to heterosexuals, especially if they had the charm and charisma Todd appeared to have had.

'One of the worst days of my life,' Bishop said, sighing. 'He was a lovely man. Always cheerful, always ready for a laugh. Gift of the gab. Paid us pretty well, looked after us. There'll never be another boss like Humph.'

'Have you any idea at all who might have wanted him dead?'

Bishop watched him in silence for some time. He was a man whose dark wavy hair was so carefully styled that it looked as if he too hadn't been keen on Bradford barbers taking the clippers to it. He had carefully tended eyebrows, dark-blue eyes and the sort of narrow moustache that put

Crane in mind of certain film actors in the old black-end-whites. He wore exactly the same clothes as Dexter, the black waistcoat and trousers, the bow tie and white shirt, but Crane suspected he added to his clothing allowance to ensure his clothes were handmade, including the perfectly fitting shirt. His bow tie too wasn't a clip-on affair, but a carefully knotted conventional one.

Bishop finally spoke. 'Well, you can't help wondering, can you?'

'What about, Gerry?'

'I … really don't know if I should say what I really think, Frank. I didn't tell the police, not that they spent too much time with me; it was mainly Pete and Helen. I was thinking of the casino, you see, and not wanting to give it a bad name.'

'In what way?'

Bishop fell silent again, touching his immaculate hair in a distracted gesture. Crane felt himself instinctively playing to the feminine traits in Bishop as if to a woman, his voice kindly and warm. He also gave out an impression that he had time and attention to spare and that he was a safe pair of hands, perhaps even giving a hint that he was charmed by the personality of the one he was dealing with.

'I'd not want any blowbacks, Frank.'

'Trust me, Gerry. I used to be in the police but I'm a private man now and nothing you can tell me will ever be tied to you.'

Crane also felt that Bishop *wanted* to tell him what he knew. Milly had told him the girls confided in him, knowing him to be both genuinely helpful and very discreet. Being the sort of man he was, he was probably proud of all the secrets and gossip he had access to, but perhaps a tiny bit galled that it all had to be kept strictly under wraps.

'Well,' Bishop said finally, 'Humph had access to some very high-grade cocaine.'

'Really. What was he doing with it, Gerry?'

'I'm pretty sure he was selling to the high-rollers. There are a lot of wealthy people in Yorkshire and they're attracted to a really nice, well-run casino like ours. You know, near the green belt, excellent cooking and a couple of tables with high mins and maxes. Well, it brings in the county folk and what rather a lot of the *gratin* fancy to get their heads into top gear is a line of the white stuff up the hooter.'

'You never saw any of it changing hands?'

'Oh God, no. Humph handled it all very discreetly because no one wants his collar felt, does he?'

'How did you find out it went on, Gerry?' he said, keeping his voice warm and friendly and devoid of the slightest hectoring note.

Bishop fingered one of his elegant jet cuff links uneasily. 'You're sure none of this will put me in it? I'd really not want The Fields to get a dodgy reputation if it got out, what with Helen struggling to cope, poor lamb. And I didn't think it would have led anywhere, really.'

'It ... might have done, Gerry,' he said quietly.

Bishop looked slightly guilty. 'Might have helped them find Humph's killer, is that what you're saying? Frank, it

was a contract killing, it couldn't have been anything else.'
He grimaced at the thought. 'You of all people, you must
know it's almost impossible pinning down a killer who does
such a horribly efficient job.'

'That's the problem with this case. But carry on.'

'Well, absolutely between you and me I got to know the
chap who was delivering the coke.'

'You *did*!'

'He came from Manchester. He had a meal here one
night, then played a little blackjack. He was gay. You
might as well know that I'm gay too. We have an instinct
for other gays and we picked up on each other. He stayed
the night at my place and well, you know … pillow talk.
He delivered for a set-up in Manchester that has access to
coke that's the equivalent of Krug. Has the same sort of
mark-up too.'

Crane was given the sort of *frisson* that came only too
rarely in his line of work. 'What was his name, Gerry? It
could be very important.'

'Liam Brent.'

'Does he still come here? I don't mean to run coke in, but
… but … well, to see you.' Crane was finding it difficult to
conceal his impatience behind the gentle, almost casual
tone.

The sadness was back in Bishop's eyes, a sadness that
seemed even more acute than when they'd talked of Todd.
'No. He stopped coming when Humph was killed. I thought
an awful lot about him. I was certain he thought the same
about me. We'd even talked of having a holiday together and

me moving to Manchester when they opened that super-duper new casino. That was before the PM put the kybosh on it.' He sighed. 'We had dreams, Liam and me. I had his mob number but when I rang the line was just dead, as if the number had been cancelled. I had his flat number but that's been dead too. I thought of going over there but his pals are dangerous people to mix with. He was hoping to get a few bob to one side and do something straight. He fancied a pub with B and B that we could run together. I just don't know what's happened to him, Frank. Maybe he's fallen for someone else.'

He looked to be close to tears now. 'It's been a double whammy these past months, Humph going, and him like a father to me, my own shit of a father scarpering when I was two years old, as they do. And then Liam taking off. To be honest I don't feel I've got a great deal to live for right now.'

Crane had his work cut out trying to hide his disappoint-ment. Liam Brent: that could have been the lead to get the case going. Drugs, a Manchester connection. Had Todd pulled some kind of a flanker on one of the Manchester barons? It happened, with that sort of loot involved. If he could have pinned down Brent he might at least have been able to prove that the mob was responsible and why; not that any single member of the mob would ever face charges, the way they watched their backs. It wouldn't have been much to take to Helen, but she had been warned not to expect much, and at least there'd be the possibility she'd know the truth. It might give her some kind of closure, in the jargon, help her to move on.

He didn't think Liam Brent had been involved in the killing, even though he'd disappeared. If he was delivering packages of cocaine he was simply a foot soldier. He was unlikely to have the skills to effect such a professional contract, and he was gay, and gays, as Crane knew, tended on the whole to steer clear of violence. 'Well, thanks for all your help, Gerry. I'm very sorry you've had all this unhappiness.'

Bishop shrugged. 'I'll get over it. I'll just have to give it time. I've got this place to keep me occupied and my old mum to keep an eye on. She's on her own, never took up with anyone else after that reptile she married slung his hook. And the girls have all been very kind to me, they know how much I thought about Humph.'

'What do you think will happen to the casino now?'

'Well, *I* think Helen should sell up. It's too much for her, managing the whole shebang.'

'Do you think Mr Romano might be interested?'

'I'm sure he would. He'd do her a fair deal too. He's a lovely man, a bit like Humph in a way. So good with people, and so generous to the girls.'

That was interesting. Both Helen and Dexter had been guarded if not uneasy when Crane had tossed Romano's name at them, but Bishop's reaction had been open and unrestrained.

'One last question, Gerry, and then I'll let you get back to the floor. You don't think anything like money laundering or skimming went on at The Fields?'

'Well … let's say we all *know* the ways money can be

made to disappear in this business, but you have to be very, very careful. If it ever came out you could lose your licence, you see, and Humph was already sailing a bit close to the wind with coke. Pete and me, we never came across anything to do with funny money, though Humph was a clever bloke.' He gave his faintly guilty smile. 'Not that we'd have blown any whistles if we had found anything dodgy, to be totally honest.'

Crane smiled, patted his arm. 'Well, thanks for everything you felt you could tell *me*.'

'You think I should have told the police, don't you?'

'Strictly speaking, yes. But I think they'd have found it as hard to do anything with it as I can.'

He could have told Bishop that in this kind of complex murder case the police always assumed that if they were managing to get at two-thirds of the truth from people they questioned they thought themselves lucky.

'I just felt I could talk to you, Frank,' Bishop said simply. 'The minute I clapped eyes on you I felt you to be a man you could trust.'

Crane could also have told him how hard he'd worked over the years to develop the dependable look of a man you could tell things to.

'Mr Romano? It's Pete Dexter.'

'Ah, Pete. Call me Alphonse, Pete. I think you and me are going to be good friends. What can I do for you?'

'It's Helen ... Alphonse. She's hired a private investigator to see if he can come up with anything about who killed

Humph. His name's Crane, Frank Crane. I thought you'd better know.'

There was a short silence at the other end of the line. 'She's gone ahead, has she? She did mention to me she was thinking of hiring a PI, with the police getting nowhere,' Romano said slowly in his deep, pleasant voice. 'I told her I thought it would be a waste of money, he'd get no further with it than the police, but she felt she had to. I can understand, Pete; she feels she has to do the best she can by poor Humph, God rest him.'

'She's desperate to know who could have done it.'

'I know, Pete, I know. What sort of man is this Frank Crane?'

'He seems pretty sharp, Mr … er … Alphonse. He's ex-CID and he knows the questions to ask. He asked about you, sir, for some reason.'

'Did he now? Why do you think that was?' Dexter caught a very faint note of disquiet in the other man's voice.

'He seemed very interested in what might happen to the casino. He asked did I think you might want to buy it.'

'How do you suppose he knew about me in the first place, Pete?'

'He picked up on you the other night when you were in. I think it was because you were playing for pretty high stakes so early in the week.'

'He doesn't miss too much, does he?'

'That's the impression I got.'

'How did you handle it, this guy asking if I might be interested in buying The Fields?'

'I played it straight, gave out that I didn't really know anything about anything.'

'That was very wise. As I said, I wish Helen hadn't taken the guy on. He'll not turn up anything worth a toss about Humph's passing, but he could get his nose poking into things that are none of his business. It worries me just a little that he's ex-CID. Once a cop always a cop. You and me, Pete, we know Humph kept a bit of coke by him for the high rollers, and we know he'll not be the only one in this business. And if he had one or two other little scams, well, we don't want any gumshoes picking up on anything and maybe not being able to stop themselves tipping off the Gaming Board or the Revenue or the police. We want to keep The Fields's impeccable image nice and intact; know what I'm saying, Pete?'

'Couldn't agree more, Alphonse. I'll keep an eye on Crane and keep you posted.'

'Well done, Pete. And you and me need to have another of our little chats before too long on that other matter. Sort out a few details, tie up the loose ends. Might be an idea if you could come over here one evening.'

'Any time, sir.'

FIVE

'Jason.'

'Frank Crane, Jase.'

'How're you doing, guv?'

'Fine. It's Humphrey Todd again, Jase. Dead casino boss.'

'What can I do for you?'

'He was into drugs, that's certain. He was bringing in top-grade coke from Manchester. Selling it to the big spenders he could depend on to keep their traps shut.'

'Should be quite a few big spenders about these days with places like Leeds and Harrogate doing so well.'

'I reckon The Fields pulls them in from a wide area. They can't drive and drink so it has to be the line up the rolled tenner. Thing is, Jase, I just have a sneaky feeling some kind of deal might have gone wrong between Todd and the Manchester boys. He just might have been the type to try and pull a fast one. You wouldn't have a Manchester contact you could have a quiet word with who'd *know* if a deal went belly-up?'

'Dodgy ground, guv. I'd have to go very, very carefully and not frighten the horses. I reckon I'd have to go over there and talk to this guy who knows that guy, well, you know the scene.'

'I know.'

'It won't be too cheap.'

'This won't be a cheap case but the lady has the folding. I've warned her it could cost. I've found out there was this bloke showing up at The Fields, a gay called Liam Brent. He was delivering the white stuff and seems to have gone missing. If I could track *him* down ...'

'Don't know I can help you there, guv. If he's gone missing he might have been in some scam with Todd, and if he was, and the big people cottoned on, Liam Brent could have been built into the footings of a new block of flats by now. I don't think I could even mention his name, too dicey. If the barons have made someone vanish it's as if he never existed. Like Joe Stalin used to say, "No man, no problem". Now if someone starts asking around about a bloke who doesn't exist it can get them very, very jumpy. And the lowlifes I'll be mixing with aren't too fussy about playing a double game. I'll do my best, guv, but—'

'OK, Jase, I understand. I certainly don't want you to put yourself in any danger. If you could just find out if anyone *had* been trying to bilk the drugs folk it would give me a motive for Todd's death and the people who arranged it.'

'Give me a couple of days, guv.'

Later that morning, Crane drove out to Cullingworth, a village in the country north-west of Bradford, hoping to catch Evelyn Cooper at home, the woman Dexter had seen having dinner with Todd not long before he died. He was pretty certain it wouldn't help the case but he'd learnt very early on never to neglect any possible lead. She lived in a large modern bungalow with extensive, well-kept gardens and there was a recent-number maroon Jaguar in the drive. Apart from giving Crane her address, Dexter had been able to confirm that the woman was married.

'Mrs Cooper?' he said as she opened the door. 'Could you spare me a few moments of your time, please?'

'I never buy anything at the door,' she said briskly, 'and I almost certainly possess any goods or services you're anxious to sell. Neither do *I* sell jewellery or *objets d'art.*'

'I'm not wanting to buy or sell anything, Mrs Cooper. I'm a private investigator working for Mrs Todd of The Fields casino. It's to do with Mr Todd's death. My name's Frank Crane.'

She gave him a hard stare but flushed slightly. 'I … don't see what Humphrey Todd's death has to do with me.'

'I believe you knew him rather well.'

'I do hope you're not implying I had anything to do with his appalling death!'

'Could we perhaps talk inside?'

She watched him warily but he had on his good blue suit and was wearing his much practised expression of pleasant inoffensiveness. 'Very well,' she said reluctantly.

She led him through to a spacious sitting room expensively furnished in a minimalist style and waved him to an armless easy chair. She sat facing him. It was spring but the mornings were still chilly and a fire of real logs glowed in a circular opening in a mottled-marble surround. A concealed music system softly played a Mozart piano concerto and there were several dramatic paintings of moorland scenes and rivers in strong brush strokes by a Yorkshire artist Crane knew to be expensive and getting more so.

'I really don't want to give you any problems, Mrs Cooper,' he said gently, 'with your husband, for example.'

'I jettisoned that piece of human garbage two years ago.'

'I see.'

'And I gamble at The Fields. I can afford to as I make a great deal of money. And yes, I was having an affair with Humph not long before he died. Does that take care of all your questions?' she said, in her clipped manner. The wary look came back into her face. 'I very much hope none of this gets back to *Mrs* Todd.'

'You have my word that it won't. When you were involved with him how did he seem?'

'Just as he always did. Funny, charming, good to be with on a night out. He was rather a special kind of man.'

He nodded sympathetically. She had high-lighted brown hair cut in an expensive and deceptively casual style. Her eyes were also brown and she had well-defined features. She was about forty but had taken great care of a good slender figure. She gave an impression of confidence and authority, even in leisure clothes of pink cable-knit sweater and dark trousers. For a couple of seconds though he'd caught the same sadness in her eyes he'd seen at times in those of Helen, Milly and Bishop.

He said, 'He gave no impression of being worried about anything?'

'No. But we business people, Mr Crane, tend to keep our worries to ourselves. Where is this leading?'

'I'm trying to find out if Mr Todd had anything on his mind, anything at all, that could lead to someone killing him, Mrs Cooper, to be blunt, which he may have … how shall I put it … unburdened himself about to you.'

'Well, there's no doubt in my mind who had a hand in Humph's death, for what it's worth. And that would be his wife.'

She spoke with such firm conviction that it threw him. 'Helen Todd? I'm *working* for Helen Todd. Believe me, she's distraught about her loss.'

'That's as may be, but the only sign of genuine uneasiness I ever saw him show was about Helen. He said to me more than once that we *had* to keep it under wraps, our thing, otherwise he could be in danger. There was no accounting what she might do.'

'Even kill him? Then pour a tanker-load of petrol in his car and set it alight?'

It wasn't easy not to smile. How many men, he wondered, had used exactly those kinds of words to ensure the new girlfriend didn't ring him at home or text his mobile? He found it difficult to believe a woman as sophisticated as Evelyn Cooper appeared to be couldn't see those warnings for exactly what they were, a way of ensuring no domestic boats were rocked.

She watched him, hard-eyed. 'I know what you're

thinking, Mr Crane. I didn't fall out of a Christmas tree. Men *do* say such things when they don't want the little woman to know. I've had other men say similar things to me, several times. But they've made no big deal about it, as I always make it crystal-clear I don't want to involve myself in any messy divorces. With Humph it was different. I could tell he was genuinely disturbed about what Helen might do if he were found out. I had an impression she might be unstable.'

'Mrs Cooper,' he said, 'take my word, Helen's devastated by her loss and I didn't see the slightest sign of instability.'

'She might well be devastated but it could quite easily be by guilt.'

'Look,' he said, 'I'm an ex-CID man. I've known domestic murders to be committed by some of the nicest women: drink, a frightful argument, a kitchen knife. A lot of women are capable of it on the spur of the moment. I could accept that even Helen Todd could do a thing like that, but to arrange an expert killing in *cold blood* ...'

'I'm not saying she had any direct involvement,' she said crisply, 'but as far as that poor man's frightful death goes all my instincts tell me that Helen Todd was in there some-where.'

'I'm sorry, Evelyn, but I really can't bring myself to believe Helen had any kind of involvement. If she had why would she hire me, a very able PI, though I say it myself?'

She was silent for some time, eyes on his but giving a preoccupied impression. When she spoke it was in a more hesitant way and not as sharply. 'I don't know ... Frank.

And I don't know why my instincts are so strong. I suppose you're right; it's not really rational, is it?'

He got up. 'I'll not take up any more of your leisure time, Evelyn. Thanks for your help. I only called because you were seeing Humph not long before he died. Frankly, I just had an idea you might possibly have a jealous husband who just might have the money and the wherewithal to arrange a professional killing. It was only ever an outside, very slim, chance but I felt I had to check it out. I'll not be troubling you again and thanks for your co-operation.'

She nodded, features suddenly heavy with a sadness she couldn't entirely control. Todd's death had brought so much pain to so many people. 'I hope you find who did it, Frank,' she said, in a low voice. 'When Humph died I'm afraid most of the colour went out of my life. It was the real thing with us, you see. Sooner or later, he told me, he'd find a way to end his marriage to a very difficult woman and spend the rest of his life with me.'

Driving back towards Bradford he guessed that Evelyn Cooper's general toughness of character still hadn't quite reached a soft and impressionable centre when she came up against a man who made more money than she did, was charismatic and great fun to be with. That had been why, though very knowing about the things married men came out with when having affairs, she'd convinced herself, on Todd's being killed, that Helen Todd had been 'in there somewhere'.

*

Bert Salter and Max Brogan were two of the men who acted as part-time inspectors when The Fields was having busy nights. They were sitting in the bar-room of a bowling club in Heaton. One was fat, one lean, one bald, one grey-haired, and both looked to be in their sixties. The fat one had an unlit pipe clenched in his teeth, the lean one an unlit cigar between his.

'Frank Crane,' Crane told them, shaking hands. 'Thanks for seeing me. Can I get you a drink?'

'No, lad, you can't, what with this being a club, do you see. You can't buy us a drink and we can't frigging well have a smoke, in case the barmaid goes home with the smell on her clothes and gives the baby lung-cancer to go with its nut allergy.'

Crane smiled, taking out a ten-pound note and slipping it to Salter. 'Well, perhaps you can buy me a drink in that case. And whatever you like for yourselves, of course. Mine's a G and T.'

'Now that's the answer, Max, eh? Very kind of you, Frank. Tessa!' Salter called, 'do an old man a favour, sweetheart, two pints of bitter and a G and T.'

'What did your last slave die of?'

'Shock. When I told him if he didn't pull his socks up I'd have him deported.'

The two men broke into a great deal of hearty laughter. Tessa brought over the drinks, raising her eyebrows to Crane but smiling. 'Well, cheers, Frank,' Brogan said. 'And what can we do for you?'

'As I said on the phone, I'm working for Helen as a PI.'

'Lovely woman, that. We're both really sorry for her,' Salter said. 'She covers it up a treat in front of the punters, but me and Max, we *know* her and we know what she's going through.'

'I agree. I've seen her away from the casino.'

'Been with Humph right back to when he had his first betting shop. She once used to do a bit of singing and dancing, you know; she was in some revival at the Alhambra one time. What was it, Max, *Salad Days?*'

'*The Boyfriend.*'

'*That*'s it. And then she got a bit part in, what was it, Max, *Last of the Summer Wine?*'

'*Emmerdale.*'

'*That*'s the one. She told me one time they were talking of making her character bigger, but by then it was all Humph and wanting to help him with his betting shop. She gave up a promising career for Humph. Mind, she's had a jolly good career anyway.'

Crane smiled patiently, waiting till he could break into the reminiscences. 'You gents help out at The Fields as inspectors?'

'That's right. Help Pete and the fairy to keep an eye on the tables,' Brogan said. 'We've both been in the gambling business all our lives.'

'Would you have any idea, any idea at all, who might have wanted him dead?'

Salter and Brogan glanced at each other warily. 'You can talk to me in total confidence,' Crane added. 'I'm not police.'

As they continued to exchange glances, he said quietly, 'I know Humph did a bit of cocaine for the big spenders.'

They both relaxed. 'We'd not want anything getting back to the police, Frank, for Helen's sake,' Salter said.

Crane said, 'You can't just go out and buy cocaine, Bert. Someone has to put you in contact with someone who deals. They have to trust you and it wouldn't just be a back-street runner. Humph was shipping in top-grade Charlie from Manchester.'

'I wonder who could have put Humph in touch with the right people, Max?' Salter said dourly. It was clear they both knew.

Crane said, 'It wouldn't be anything to do with a Mr Alphonse Romano, by any chance?'

The two men watched him for some time in silence. Finally Salter said, 'We always felt he was getting a bit too close to the Eyetie.'

'The gambling business can be a rough old game, Frank,' Brogan said. 'You need to be tough and you need your wits about you to make a go of it. Well, Romano's something else. His folks settled in the UK after the war and we reckon they came from the wrong end of Italy.'

'He's a charming bloke, Frank, you can't help liking him. Gave me and Max a bottle each of twelve-year single malt last Christmas, said he wished he could get part-timers as good as us in Scarborough. He's got this casino well out of the town and countrified, like The Fields. He didn't want no riff-raff coming straight in off the front and wanting to play the tables in T-shirts. He wanted a better class of punter, just like Humph. Middle-class folk, toffs and so forth. He was never away from The Fields at one stage. Me and Max think he was picking Humph's brains. Well, I mean Humph had everything spot on, hadn't he, the restaurant, the lighting, the way the girls were kitted out? Mind you, Humph had a lot of time for him, both him and Helen. They thought he was a great guy.'

'We hinted he needed watching, Frank,' Brogan went on. 'We're old men and we know a hell of a lot of people in the game. We reckon he runs his Scarborough place as a kind of flagship. It's run very carefully but we've heard he's got other clubs and casinos, rough-end city ones where he's got as many scams going as the fingers on your hands: drugs, skimming, laundering, call-girls. We dropped a hint to Humph about Romano's scams; said maybe best not to get too close, but he just said in this business who didn't have scams? He didn't want to know and we decided it wasn't really any of our business. But it was pretty bloody certain it was the Eyetie got him his drug connection.'

Crane said, 'He's still coming over to The Fields, even though Humph's dead. Why's that, do you suppose?'

'He's the sort of bloke who doesn't do anything without a good reason,' Salter said.

'What reason do you think that might be?'

'Helen might want to sell up. It's too much to cope with on her own.'

Crane nodded. It kept coming back to the possibility of Helen selling up. 'You say both Humph *and* Helen got on with Romano. You don't think Helen and Romano...?'

'No chance. She liked the attention, that southern charm, what woman wouldn't? But it was never anyone but Humph. Well, you're working for her; you've seen the state she's in when she's not on parade.'

Crane finished his drink, got up. 'Well, thanks for your help, gentlemen, it could be useful.'

'Romano's into scams, Frank, and we're certain he got Humph the drugs connection, but he'll not have had anything to do with the poor sod buying it.'

'Not his style. Whatever he wants from folk he just charms it out of them.'

Crane drove next to Terry Jones's place on Bingley Road. He was in the back garden, clearing winter detritus from the borders.

'Frank! Good to see you. How're you doing?'

'Fine. And you? Just a quick word, Terry. I don't want to keep you away from your heavy digging.'

Jones flicked his head back. 'You can keep me away from it all bleeding day, pal. I'm under orders from 'er indoors. Fancy a yardarmer?'

'I'd better not. I'm having to have the odd drink in the line of duty and I don't want to overdo it.'

Jones led him to a bench set beneath a sycamore tree at the bottom of the garden. The day was beginning to warm up and it was pleasant to sit in the sunlight and the fresh spring air.

'Getting anywhere with the Todd carry-on?'

'You didn't hear this from me, Terry, but he was into

drugs. Top-grade coke that he sold to top-grade members he could trust.'

'Was he now? We suspected it, the way he died, but no bugger would let on. So what's new? As you can guess we weren't pulling out too many stops, with it having gangland written all over it. Even so, we did pick up some DNA.'

'You did?'

'We reckon the gunman had a drag to calm his nerves at some point. We did a fingertip in the immediate area and picked up on the dog-end. The forensics managed to get a reading.'

'Maybe the butt was Todd's?'

'We took that into account. Helen gave us a hair from Todd's hairbrush and it ruled him out.'

'You couldn't match it, of course.'

Jones sighed. 'Christ, there must be upward of five million DNA readings on the national database, all taken from crime suspects however minor the crime. Best thing since sliced bread as far as the police are concerned. But no, we couldn't match the sod. I suppose it's unlikely a real pro of a killer *would* have his DNA in the system anyway.'

Crane nodded, but wondered all the same if a real pro would leave behind even a cigarette end. Real pros tended to have a mind for that kind of detail, as he knew from a former case where a contract killer had been involved.

Jones took in Crane's glum expression. The poor guy was beating himself up as usual because he looked to be getting nowhere. He was no different from the way he'd been in the force: dedicated, unsparing of himself, working the clock round to get a result. Jones was certain if Crane could get nowhere with Todd's killer no one could.

'Sorry I've nothing for your comfort, Frank.'

'I didn't honestly think you would have. The real reason I called, I had an idea there might be an outside chance of Todd having some kind of a run-in with the Manchester drugs people.'

He told Jones what he'd learned from Bishop, about Liam Brent bringing in the cocaine but later disappearing. 'I've got a contact who might be able to find out if one of the drug barons found himself a few bob short. It would provide a motive for Todd's death, at least.'

Jones grinned. 'The sort of contact who knows how to hack his way into folks' bank accounts and share portfolios?'

Crane also grinned. 'I daresay his various skills wouldn't be entirely unadjacent to those kinds of activities. Anyway, this guy isn't keen about asking around about Liam Brent in case it becomes too dangerous.'

'I might be able to help there,' Jones said slowly. 'There's a chap in the Manchester force I speak to. I'll ask him if any of the CID people have a reliable snout who can confirm this Brent bloke's off the scene. I can see where you're coming from. If Brent's gone to ground he may have seen off Todd himself. If he's dead he could have been part of Todd's scam. If there *was* a scam.'

'That's about it, Terry. If you can find out if Brent's gone to ground or been quietly put down and my bloke can confirm that a drug deal went belly-up I can go back to Helen and tell her it's ninety per cent certain Brent or the mob killed Humph. She won't like it but at least she'll *know*.'

'And our Manchester friends will be keen to nail Brent if he's alive, even if the murder was on our patch. I daresay they'll already know about him being a carrier.'

'Thanks a lot, Terry. I owe you.'

'No problem. Just glad we plods can help you clever private men.'

He gave an ironic smile, but the trouble was though, when he was around Frank Crane, with his rapid brain, his drive, his doggedness and his flashes of intuition, Inspector Jones often did feel a bit of a plod.

SIX

She sounded drowsy. 'Big night at The Fields?' he asked. 'It's Frank Crane, Milly.'

'God, Sunday's my crashing-*out* day! Don't you ever do crashing-out days?'

'I'd maybe have one if I could ever see the end of my workload.'

'What do you *want*?'

'I was hoping I could take you to the Fox for a drink and a bite of lunch. But if you've got other plans ...'

'You're in luck. I can just find a window in my crowded appointments diary. Yes, I'd rather like to go to the Fox. Give me half an hour. I should be well out of my *déshabillé* by then.'

'I really wouldn't mind if you were still *in* your *déshabillé*.'

'Can I really take the risk, I ask myself, of going to the Fox with a smooth-talking bastard like you?'

Smiling, Crane closed his mobile and set off to drive across the city to Milly's place. He was catching up on routine work that was being neglected because of the time he was giving to the Todd case. But it would be nice to take a woman to lunch, especially one who looked like Milly. He guessed that if she could find the time to go to lunch with him on her day off there was no regular bloke hanging about. Which maybe confirmed that she'd been another of Todd's girlfriends and, like Evelyn Cooper, was still trying to get over him. And hadn't she admitted, the first time he'd taken her to lunch, that she was still trying to come to terms with the death of someone close?

'Hi, Frank.' She was wearing one of her roll-neck sweaters, pink this time, striped cord jeans and a short woollen jacket in oatmeal. Ideal clothes for bright sunny weather that still had a nip in the air. She was lightly made up but her face still had that slightly ethereal pale colouring that made such a startling contrast to the vivid features Helen insisted the croupier girls displayed.

'You look very nice,' he said, taking her to his car.

'Thank you. You can't imagine the relief it is to look normal after being painted up to look like someone who should be draped round a pole.'

He wondered if he detected a note of distaste for the image she had to project at the casino, even though she'd told him she was a night person who got off on running a table.

He bought drinks at the Fox and Grapes and they studied the extensive Sunday lunchtime menu chalked on a blackboard. Milly ordered scrambled eggs and smoked salmon and Crane a ham sandwich. They then carried their drinks out to the beer garden, already busy in the clear light and occasional shadow of a day of drifting cloud.

'This is nice,' Milly said, looking round wistfully, as if a pub lunch in a beer garden was something that she experienced only rarely, if at all.

'What do you usually do on Sundays?'

'Not a lot. I really do feel the need to recharge the batteries.'

To Crane, it seemed a very dull existence for a young woman, apart from the absorbing hours she spent at the casino. But could *any* woman really want to do it for anything but the money?

'I'd have thought there were blokes standing in line wanting to take you out.'

She smiled, shrugged. 'It can be difficult finding someone who isn't rather put off by the work I do.'

'Does that go for the other girls?'

'They're mainly married or in relationships. They tend to be working hard with partners to afford a mortgage.'

Crane could see that that would be worth the sacrifice of decent leisure time, but Milly appeared to have a house of her own. In fact she gave an impression of being comfortably off, judging by her newish motor and good-quality clothes.

'Your invite to lunch came as a pleasant surprise,' she said, 'but I get a strong impression there might be an ulterior motive lurking in there with a man as driven as you.'

He smiled. 'I'll put my hand up. There's a man called

Alphonse Romano who was at The Fields the first night I came.'

'We all know him well. He's very good with the girls, big tips, friendly manner.'

'I get the feeling he might like to buy The Fields.'

'There has been a rumour.'

'I'd like to check out his own place, near Scarborough.'

She watched him for a short time in silence. 'You can't think he had anything to do with—'

'I'm a PI, Milly, who used to be a cop. I tick all the boxes in a difficult case like this, not to let anything go by default. It can waste me a lot of time, but that's the nature of the job.'

'Where do I come in?'

'I don't suppose you could take a day off?'

Her eyes widened slightly. 'It's … possible …'

'Could you come to Scarborough with me? Tomorrow, if that wouldn't be too difficult. I'd like to visit Romano's place. If we went as a couple it would improve my cover.'

'But you're not a member, are you?'

Crane cursed inwardly, angry with himself for over-looking a crucial detail. He'd have to be a member and would almost certainly have to wait twenty-four hours before he could enter the gaming room. He shook his head.

'Nor me. And visits to one casino while employed by another means I'd face instant dismissal if it came to light.' She sipped some of her vodka and coke. 'We could join, I suppose. I doubt the reception people would associate me with The Fields.'

'We'd have to make sure Romano himself didn't spot you.'

'I doubt he'd know me, out of war paint and glad rags.'

'That's a good point.'

'How would it work? Drive there tomorrow evening, join the casino, then go back the following day?'

'It's a bit messy, but we can have a decent meal on the way back.'

She smiled, and the slight heaviness that never quite left her eyes briefly lifted. 'Sounds as if it could be quite fun.'

'You'll help me? I really don't know what I'll be looking for but I'd appreciate your reactions to Romano's set-up.'

She nodded. 'I really would like to see someone punished for Humph's death. For Helen's sake. She puts a brave face on it but I can almost feel her pain.'

Crane guessed she'd be sensitized to pain when she was in pain herself for 'someone close' who'd died.

'Ah,' he said, as the waitress appeared, 'our food. Can I get you a glass of wine?'

'Please.' Milly found herself looking forward to a trip to Scarborough with Frank Crane. It made a change to be looking forward to anything.

'Pete? It's Alphonse. Is that detective guy still hanging about?'

'It all seems to have gone quiet. I shouldn't be surprised if he's on the point of packing it in. What *could* he come up with? I reckon even the bogies have written it off as a contract. Who do you reckon could have fixed the contract, Alphonse?'

'It's got to be one of the Manchester people, Pete. You and me, we know he was dealing the best coke you could lay hands on. Those guys have a lot of pull in Colombia. Humph was a lovely bloke, God rest him, and a very, very clever one, but if he got across the drugs people they settle things very quickly. Well, it can be a dangerous game. I doubt anyone's ever going to know who put the poor guy in an urn. How's Helen holding up?'

'She's soldiering on but she knows it's too much for her, running the whole caboodle. I reckon she's just about ready to think about selling up.'

'Another fortnight, Pete, then I'll make her an offer she'll find it very hard to refuse.' He chuckled. 'Which reminds me, you and me, we need to talk very soon. I've thought up a little package I'm hoping you too will find hard to refuse.'

Crane drove steadily towards the coast. As he had time to spare, he took what he called the top route, past Ripon and Thirsk and through the Hambleton Hills, where you climbed a long steep gradient in second, called Sutton Bank, and where at the summit you felt you were driving on top of the world, with farmland spread out far below and stretching into a distant blue mist. They didn't talk much but he sensed her alertness to the scenery and the dramatic rays of evening sun through broken cloud, covering the terrain in a sharp-edged mosaic of light and shade. He could tell she was relieved not to be going to The Fields tonight.

Still on the A170 and on the outskirts of Scarborough, they saw it, a fine square mansion standing well back from the road and backed by rising land and forest trees. A wall encircled it, with a discreet wooden sign near open iron gates that simply said 'Romano's'.

'Why out here?' Milly said. 'I'd have thought all the action was down on South Bay.'

'He's doing a Humph Todd. He doesn't want the T-shirts with a few crumpled fivers in their jeans, he wants the carriage trade who drive out and have a nice meal and do some serious punting. Wealthy people retire to those villages we drove through. I reckon that wealthy blokes who've been hot-shots in the boardroom find themselves bored out of their skulls at times and start to think in terms of Romano's.'

And if Romano had a nice line in discreet call-girls and the white stuff that would be all to the good, Crane thought. As if to bear out his words the car park contained a considerable poundage of high-quality wheels. It was mid-evening by now with the light almost gone. A well-dressed woman sat in reception and a strong-looking man stood to one side in evening clothes, the obligatory bouncer that even the most well-run of casinos seemed unable to do without. Crane and Milly completed simple forms and produced their driving-licence photocards as proof of identity and address. They were treated very politely as they were both dressed carefully from the better end of their wardrobes.

'The amenities of the club will be available in twenty-four hours, sir and madam,' the woman said. 'You'll be fully registered by then.'

'Thank you,' Crane said, 'we're looking to come back tomorrow evening.'

'We'll look forward to welcoming you, Mr Crane.'

They walked back to Crane's car. 'Hungry, Milly?'

'I am rather.'

'We'll find somewhere on the way back.' He glanced at the car clock. 'But time's passing on. It might be as well if we went on to Scarborough. There's a hotel on St Nicolas Street that's reliable.'

'It *would* be nice to see the lights and the sea. I've not been to the coast for such a long time.'

Three hours later they sat over a final drink in Milly's hotel room.

When they'd driven into Scarborough Crane had parked on St Nicholas Cliff, then they'd walked to the nearby Royal and were able to have dinner there. The dining room had the sort of stateliness that now went with only a handful of the very old seaside hotels, with wall lights and chandeliers, pillars and ornate plaster moulding. A piano tinkled in the background.

'One up on a pub supper,' he said.

A busy waiter handed them menus and a wine list and darted off again. 'I'd better order wine by the glass,' Crane said. 'I'm kind of paranoid about not going over the limit. No car, no job.'

'It would have been nice if you could have relaxed over a bottle of wine. Oh well …'

Without thinking, he said, 'We could stay over, I suppose.

The season hasn't got going. I'm sure they'd have a couple of rooms.'

'Do you mean it? I can afford it if you can.'

'Why not. But I'll pay. Can't have you out of pocket for helping me out.'

'We'll argue about who pays what later, but I really would love to stay,' she said, almost eagerly. 'I've not done anything like this since—' She abruptly broke off. Since when, he wondered. Since Humphrey Todd had stolen a few hours with her in some other hotel? 'Since last summer, I *think*,' she added after a moment.

'What will you do about not showing up at The Fields?'

'I'll pull a sicky,' she said, smiling, 'to quote the machine-shop girls in *Coronation Street.*'

They gave the waiter their choices for dinner and Crane ordered a half of Chablis for the fish and a bottle of Médoc for the main course.

She said, 'And we go back in the morning?' It was more a question than a statement.

'Or we could spend a day in Scarborough and go back tomorrow night after Romano's.'

'How could you *possibly* spend a day away from your work?'

'An old biddy called Maggie works for me a couple of hours a day. She'll rejig my schedule. She's used to my irregular existence. Maybe I deserve a day off as I don't do holidays. Maybe we both do.'

It was good to see the pleasure she took in the long leisurely meal, chatting of this and that: films, books, current affairs. She was well-read and intelligent and he couldn't help thinking once again that she belonged more in an office with a clearly defined future than at a gambling table where her career could end when her looks faded. He left her for a short time during coffee to see about rooms. There were two singles available. 'We're in,' he said, back at the table. 'I'm sorry you'll not have any nightwear.'

'I'll cope,' she said, smiling. 'Once winter's over I sleep in the buff anyway. You'll be in the same boat.'

'I keep an overnight bag permanently in the car. I've got a spare toothbrush I can let you have. Unused, I hasten to add!'

It had been a good evening and they now sat in Milly's room sipping sparkling water. She knew he'd not try anything on, even though perhaps she'd not really have minded. You could never tell with men, but there was something about Crane that she was certain meant that what you saw was what you got. She said, 'The first time we went for a drink you said you had no wife or partner. Does that mean no one at all?'

'Not exactly. I have a friend. We have what you could call a semi-detached or open relationship. She has her own place and I have mine and we see each other maybe once a week. We both carry a fair amount of baggage, both work silly hours and neither wants to be tied.'

'Sounds a sensible arrangement.'

'It suits the sort of people we are. How about you? I know you've had an upset. Someone close dying ...'

She sipped a little from her glass and gazed past him

with unfocused eyes. She was silent for some time, as if trying to decide whether or not to admit to what he was certain was the case, that she too had been involved with Humphrey Todd.

'It ... wasn't a boyfriend,' she said at last. 'It was my sister, Sophie. She died not very long ago.'

'Oh, I'm so sorry ...'

'We were very close. My dad's a professional army man. He's always been very ambitious, always ready to take a new posting. We were always on the move, leaving friends behind, trying to make new ones. In the end, Sophie and me, we were simply each other's best friend. Then Mum and Dad decided we needed permanence, proper schooling. It was arranged we'd stay with Mum's sister and her husband. We didn't much like it; they had a son and daughter of their own who resented us. It brought us even closer. As soon as we were working we left, rented a flat. We ended up in the house in Highgate. Dad helped us get on what they call the housing ladder. He was always generous financially, it was just his time, and Mum's, that tended to be in short supply.'

'And then she died on you. It must have been a dreadful blow.'

'Most sisters get on, but Sophie and me, we'd *always* been together.' She smiled faintly. 'We two against the world, to use the old cliché. She was like part of me, like an identical twin.'

'How did she die? But look, if it's too upsetting—'

'If she *did* have to die I wish so much it *could* have been an illness or a car accident.' There was another lengthy silence. 'One night she went to a house in Hawksworth. A big detached house ... isolated. No one knows how she ended up there. But there were several men there and just Sophie. She was given a spiked drink at some point that made her confused and then she was raped. A number of times.'

'Oh, *Milly* ...'

'She was badly injured ... internally. The men cleared off. But the Jacuzzi had been set going and Sophie ... she was badly hurt ... groggy. She fell in the Jacuzzi and drowned. That's ... that's how the police saw it anyway.'

Crane remembered now. The evening paper had given it a lot of coverage and the nationals had also picked up on it. He couldn't recall any arrests.

'They ... never caught anyone?'

She shook her head. 'The owner of the house was away. He has no idea who the men were. They must have got in by a French window he'd forgotten to lock. It was ajar.'

'There'd be DNA, wouldn't there? Fingerprints?'

'Plenty of DNA,' she said, eyes beginning to brim with tears. 'But the police, they couldn't match any of it with the database.'

'I'm so very sorry, Milly,' he said gently. He put a hand on her arm. 'But the police must have profiled Sophie's lifestyle.'

'She was working in a restaurant.' She spoke in an almost strangled tone through her sobs. 'She was hoping to make a career in catering. No one ... no one has any idea where she went when she left the restaurant. We ... we just had the one car between us and I needed it that night; she said she'd come home in a cab. No one has any idea how she ended up in the Hawksworth house.'

Her moist eyes rested on his, heavy now with the sadness she'd always seemed to carry a trace of around with her. She dabbed them with a tissue. 'She was older than me, but it always seemed to be me keeping an eye on *her*. She was great fun, loved pulling the blokes, we'd go on the pull together and I'd make sure she didn't get involved with the wrong types. She was naïve, a bit too trusting, that was the trouble, but she was never … never a scrubber. The police accepted that in the end. She may have hooked up with someone she knew I'd not approve of and was keeping it quiet.'

She'd dried her eyes and was speaking in a more controlled way now. 'The CID people came to our house, checking her room for clues, a diary, though I knew she didn't keep one. They got nowhere. What they did say was that they couldn't see the men being the sort of petty criminals they dealt with every day, otherwise they'd almost certainly have matched a fingerprint or some DNA. And they can't see how the men knew the house would be unoccupied. But the owner knew absolutely nothing about it, he was up in the Lakes when it happened.'

Crane nodded. 'They've got a tough job on their hands if none of the men had any form or any DNA that could be matched. And it's pretty obvious it's a conspiracy of silence. It *could* be solved one day by one of the men breaking the law in some other way, having his DNA routinely taken and it then being found to link to Sophie, but I'm afraid that would be a very long shot, though it does happen now and then. That's why the police wish to God the entire population had their DNA on the database.'

'They told me not to give up hope; they'll not let it go.' She shrugged. 'But ... well, it won't bring her back, will it? She'll be completely forgotten soon, my sister, my closest friend. Except by me.'

'And your mum and dad.'

'They more or less forgot us years ago.'

Such sad words. They weren't true; they'd be grieving in their own way, but there was a grain of truth. Children who were separated from their parents, for however worthy the motives, nearly always seemed to resent it, to feel rejected. Looking back on his own happy childhood he supposed that, in Milly's shoes, he'd have felt the same.

'You must be very lonely,' he said, 'on your own in the house you bought together.'

'I'm learning to live with it,' she said, sighing. 'We shared everything, Frank: money, holidays, nights out, the cooking and cleaning. We used to say that when we did get married we'd have to stipulate that we lived in the same area. I doubt that would have been possible, but if we'd had to live a long way apart we'd have fretted. As I've found out these past months.'

'You need a decent bloke, Milly, to help you get over her. If I were you I'd pack it in at the casino very soon and get a job with decent hours, so you've got the time to *meet* a decent bloke. You're too good for gambling joints, however upmarket.'

She gave him a pleased smile, as if glad he'd seen so much more in her than did the men who gathered round her table, lasciviously eyeing the enamelled piece of totty they imagined her to be in the enhancing key light. 'You're right,' she said. 'Mum hates the idea of me working there. That's when she's actually in England for a couple of days.'

He smiled, glanced at his watch. 'I'd better be going down the corridor.'

She got up from her chair and moved towards the window, on which the curtains were still undrawn, with her glass. 'I should think the view from here's lovely in daylight.'

'You should be able to see the sea beyond St Nicholas Cliff.'

'I'd ... I'd rather you stayed. As long as your semi-detached girlfriend doesn't come along one day and boil my rabbits.'

He watched her where she stood in the light of table lamps, elegant in pleated skirt and cashmere cardigan, brown wavy hair falling to her shoulders. She turned round slowly. He said, 'I'll stay with you, Milly, if it's what you want and we both accept it would just be a one-off.'

'I'll be in a strange bed in a strange town and I've just had a bad half-hour, even though I'm glad you let me talk about it. I suppose the wine made me emotional. I'd just like a little company.'

'I'll be back.'

He went to his own room to get his overnight bag. He didn't do casual sex these days, not since taking up with

Colette, but the kid was vulnerable and he felt sorry for her. And he was also convinced she grieved for two people, both Sophie and Humphrey Todd, both dying in the most appalling way. Why would a bright young woman with a good job in the public sector want to pack it in for an insecure one in the gaming business with unsocial hours unless Todd had been involved? He guessed she'd been flattered by the attention he must have shown her at that first dinner she'd gone to with her friends from the Revenue. Yet that didn't really fit with the sensible impression she'd given him of being the more level-headed of the two sisters. He gave a shrug. What did they say, the heart has its reasons? But just now she wanted comfort sex and he'd had a fair amount of experience in that line.

But when he took her naked body in his arms she said, in a low voice. 'I'm sorry, Frank, will you just hold me? I can't seem to get my mind round sex right now. I'm very sorry. Go back to your own bed if you'd rather.'

'That's all right, I'll just hold you,' he said. It was frustrating, now he was in bed with an attractive woman, but he felt he could see it from the lonely tragic place she lived in, a dead sister, a possible dead lover. He supposed a woman of her sensibilities might see sex as providing no real answer to the many long, tear-stained nights she'd recently lived through.

So he held her in the coastal silence, inhaling the scent of a body that smelt so different from Colette's, which was all he'd known this past couple of years. He hoped she *would* find a man one day who'd help her to live again the sort of life he felt she so much longed for, a release from the void left by Sophie and Todd.

She suddenly gave a little shake and made a sound that could have been either a sob or a giggle.

'Milly...?

She made the same sound again; it was definitely a giggle. 'Oh, I suddenly remembered the nights when me and Soph would go out on the pull. She could be so funny about some of the men who'd try their luck. She'd think I was out of my tree, being here in bed with a decent bloke like you and not ... and not ...'

'Does that mean you're considering more than just holding?'

'I think Sophie would have had a point.'

Later, she kissed him on the cheek and whispered, 'Thank you, Frank, that made me feel I was beginning to get back into the land of the living.'

The sun shone through breaks in rapidly moving cloud and there was a stiff breeze from an unsettled sea. As they walked along Foreshore Road the tide was pounding against the sea wall and sending gouts of glittering spray fifteen or twenty feet in the air to fall on to the opposite deserted pavement.

'Not just high tide,' Crane told her, 'but a high *spring* tide. I remember it well as a boy. Naturally I'd go as near the wall as I dared and run like hell when the next wave came. I didn't always win.'

She smiled, her eyes gleaming in the hard light. She'd

earlier gone into the shopping centre not far from the hotel and bought herself a parka and some track-shoes. Crane already had those sort of clothes in the boot of his car. She said, 'With all this light and wind and water I feel as if my brain's having a clear-out.'

'It needs one, Milly, all the trouble you've known.'

She gazed out over the churning sea, the wheeling gulls and the tidal fountains. 'It's like a day out of normal life, a good day for making a new start.'

'That's it. A completely fresh page for Miss Emilia Brown.'

They paused, to watch the activity in Old Harbour. Looking around her, she suddenly gave a start, her face paling, her mouth falling open. She grasped his arm and tried to speak but nothing came out.

'What is it, Milly? Not feeling so good?'

'It's ... it's all right.' She got out the words with an effort. 'I've seen a ghost, that's all.' She peered back along the front, busy with trippers. He could feel her hand shaking. 'Can these things *happen?*' she gasped. 'That you get a sudden glimpse ... an impression ... of someone close ... even though they've gone ...'

He put an arm round her. 'She's been on your mind a lot. You were so upset about her last night. You told me all about her. Then you see someone who bears a resemblance ...'

She still gazed at the knots of strolling people as if still searching for the face that must have triggered the memory of her sister. 'I'm sure you're right,' she said, 'I must be in a suggestible state.'

'The mind can play funny tricks.'

They walked on, past Luna Park and round Castle Hill, then, skirting North Bay, they hiked along the cliffs to a village called Burniston, where they had a pub lunch. For some time, after seeing what seemed to have been an apparition of Sophie, she walked in a subdued silence. She began to regain her spirits in the wind that tousled her hair and brought the colour to her cheeks, and in the sweeping views they'd often pause to take in from the Cleveland Way of a turbulent sea over rocky inlets. She began to talk cheerfully then of the places she and Sophie had seen on their father's postings, the towns they'd lived in, the excursions they'd made.

Back in Scarborough, she put a hand on his arm. 'It's been a long, long time, Frank, since I've spent a day I've enjoyed so much.'

They'd checked out of their hotel but went back for an early dinner. Crane then drove to Romano's, both now wearing once again the formal clothes they'd worn the evening before. He parked among the expensive motors and they went in the casino through the imposing main entrance. The elegant woman in reception had the sort of memory that went with the job in such a well-run operation. 'Ah, Mr Crane and Ms Brown. Good evening and welcome. I have your cards here. If you'd be good enough to sign them in front of me everything will then be in order.'

The big man in evening clothes, who looked capable of splitting a brick in two with the edge of a hand, wasn't around this time, but Crane guessed he could be summoned in part of a second if anyone of the wrong type attempted to bluff his way, cardless, on to the gambling floor.

They signed their cards and were then ushered to a door that opened on to a short corridor that led to the bar and restaurant.

'Enjoy your evening,' the woman said, 'and good luck.'

Crane bought drinks. The bar area gave on to the restaurant in a way that showed a close resemblance to The Fields. Not only that but the restaurant itself looked to be a near-exact replica of The Fields: the same picture lights above the same sorts of dreamy Impressionist prints in gold frames, the same shade of deep carpeting, the same kinds of cutlery and glass, the napkins even carefully ironed into fan shapes. Fresh flowers stood on antique pieces of furniture which occupied similar positions against the walls.

'We could be at The Fields,' Milly said, in a wondering tone.

'Romano obviously liked the way Humph had done his.'

Crane remembered seeing the way Romano had continually glanced round the gambling room at The Fields when the roulette wheel was revolving, in that odd appraising way. He'd wondered later, when he'd discovered who Romano was, if it could have been the calculating look of a man trying to decide how much the casino was worth. Well, it could have been, but he was beginning to think there was more to it. He was impatient now to see the floor. They finished their drinks then went down the few steps that led on to the floor, just as those at The Fields did. Milly came to an abrupt halt at the foot of the steps, mouth falling open a little, as if she'd seen another ghost. 'Are we in some kind of a time warp? It *is* The Fields! It's exactly the same. Exactly.'

It was uncanny. There was scarcely a pin's difference between the two casinos. The layout was identical: the same planters standing in the same spots, with the same gleaming leaves of some exotic species, the same clever lighting plan, the same key lights that enhanced the sleek heads of the same type of dazzling, smiley, carefully made-up croupier girls.

She gazed at him, wide-eyed. 'What does it mean, Frank? Why has he made such an exact imitation of Humph's place?'

'I don't know, Milly. He must have been very impressed by the things Humph had done.'

'They must qualify as two of the finest casinos in the north. I daresay the cooking will be just as good as at The Fields too.'

'You're right. Both places outside of town in fine old houses, pulling in some of Yorkshire's wealthiest punters,' he said, as they moved slowly round the tables, as if deciding at which to play.

'Do you think that's why he might want to buy The Fields?'

'I'm suddenly certain of it,' he said, returning the friendly smile of a black-waistcoated patrolling inspector. 'Between you and me, Milly, Romano comes over as a pretty shady character. I had it from Bert and Max, the part-time inspectors at The Fields, yes? And if Romano owned *two* casinos of the calibre of his own and The Fields it would give him an awful lot of respectability to hide his dodgy dealings behind: drugs, laundering, call-girls.' He spoke softly but there was a good deal anyway of background noise on the floor: the rattling balls, the clicking of counters as bets were paid out or swept in, the low hum of conversation.

'Can you be *sure* he does things like that? He seems to be such a nice, charming bloke.'

'I've always been uneasy with charm. I've seen the ugly side it can often have. Look, I'm talking off the top of my head now but the government was planning to license a big Las Vegas-style casino in Manchester, but then they pulled the plug on the idea. But another part of the plan was to give the go-ahead to about sixteen smaller casinos in other towns and cities. I'm not sure but I think that part of the scheme might still be in place. What if Romano could get himself granted one of *those* licences, to set up, say, at some-where like Harrogate or Wetherby? He looks to be a very ambitious man; he could end up controlling most of the gambling in the county, either in his own name or through front men. And with his charm and apparent respectability and his perfectly run casinos he'd come to be regarded as a safe pair of hands. I've absolutely no doubt he donates heavily to whichever party is in power. But first, maybe he needs to get his hands on Humph's place because it's begin-ning to look obvious that it was Humph who showed him how to make big money out of gambling by getting the right property and the right ambience.'

They sat at a table that wasn't too busy and Crane

bought low-value chips to put down on even chances and columns. Milly said, 'Do you think he may have tried to buy out Humph earlier?'

'It could very well be. And maybe Humph didn't want to know. Maybe Humph had similar ambitions of his own.'

'You don't think,' she whispered, 'that Romano really *could* have … that night at the driving place…?'

'Not his style, so I've been told. But there could be *some* sort of connection between Romano and Humph's death. The trouble is, it was such an expert killing and left no traces.'

But could the killer have been a genuine contract man, he wondered, who'd smoke a cigarette then throw the stub into the long grass? He sighed. 'How will we ever know *who* killed him unless I get very lucky?' He glanced at his watch. 'Well, I think we might as well hit the road home. Apart from Romano stealing all Humph's ideas to use in his own place, I don't think that there's going to be anything else that gives me any real help. As I said before, I'd no real idea what I'd expected to *find*.'

But he was then to find something that could be very important indeed. They'd been sitting at a table towards the top of the room among well-dressed men and women who looked to have eaten well and had the sort of wealth that would be largely unaffected by any money they might win or lose tonight. Romano himself hadn't been around. Crane had noted what seemed to be the single difference between Romano's and The Fields. Romano's actually ran to a *salon privé*, where the really big spenders could play to much higher limits than on the floor. As they got up to go, a waitress was approaching the *salon privé* with a tray on which stood three drinks. As she knocked and pushed open the door, Crane had a couple of seconds before it swung shut to glimpse three men sitting at a roulette table in a room that was otherwise not in use. They had almost literally their heads together. One of the men was Romano, another was his evening-suited minder and the man sitting between the two was Pete Dexter.

SEVEN

Crane drove up from Cross Flatts to Moor Rise, with its elegant gabling and its emerald lawns, spring flowers and budding ornamental trees. The housekeeper led him into the same spacious room Helen had seen him in before. It had an unlived-in look. The expensive tables and cabinets gleamed, there were fresh flowers in vases, books on bookshelves, but there seemed to be no homely touches that would give it warmth, no crumpled newspapers lying about, no slippers by the fireside, no empty cups or glasses, the sorts of things that tended to lie about in Crane's living room.

Helen Todd sat on a sofa in her dark clothes, her pale face and dark-shadowed eyes giving their usual impression of endless grief when she was away from work. It seemed a pity the Todds hadn't had children, who'd now be able to support her in the long empty days she was living through. Maybe ambition had come before children, as it sometimes did.

'Hello, Frank, sit down. Coffee? Would you mind, Ginny.'

The housekeeper went off. 'Well, Frank, any news?'

'Nothing definite, but I'm working on a couple of leads. And I'm afraid it may come as something of a shock to you but it seems Humph was involved in drugs.'

'Drugs!' she cried. '*Drugs!* I never knew anything about drugs. Whatever makes you think that?'

'He was getting high-grade cocaine from some people in Manchester and … well, selling it, I suppose, to wealthy members he could trust.'

Her mouth fell open slightly. 'Oh, Frank, can you be sure? Who told you this?'

He hesitated. 'I … got the information in confidence, Helen. All I can say is that I trust my source.'

'Drugs,' she almost whispered. 'I'd no idea, I'd really no idea. Not at The Fields. I'd always wanted it to be exclusive, above anything like that.'

'I doubt it affected the standing of the club, not with the sort of people who can afford to buy this top-quality stuff. As far as I can understand, at the wealthy end of society it tends to beat alcohol these days as the leisure drug of choice. The trouble is it can be a dangerous business to be involved in if things go wrong.'

'How do you mean, if things go wrong?' She spoke almost vaguely as if still trying to cope with the shock of the new revelation.

'This is difficult for me, Helen, but Humph might have had some sort of dispute with the drugs people. I'm afraid they tend to settle disputes very quickly and often in the way Humph was killed.'

'But the police—'

'They've always felt gangland people were involved. And I'm going to have to tell you, and I may know for near-certain very soon, that if these people *did* kill Humph it'll be virtually impossible to track down exactly which person actually did it.'

She nodded slowly, gazing past Crane without focus. Then her eyes began to brim with tears that glinted in the band of sunlight she was sitting in. She brushed them away with the back of a hand, gave a half-sob. 'I'm … I'm sorry, Frank,' she said, in a thin, strained tone. 'I don't like not being in control. It's just that when I get … get talking about him. And … and no one ever likely to pay for what they've done to him. He meant so much to me. Well … he was my life.'

Crane was sitting on a nearby chair. He put a hand on her arm. He was doing a lot of comforting just now. He gave himself regular warnings to be objective, not to get emotionally involved by the distress Helen and Milly had had to take on board, Helen for Todd and Milly for both Todd and the sister who'd been like another self. 'I'm sorry, Helen, Humph being gone is more than enough to cope with without having to hear these unpleasant details.'

She nodded wanly, grasped the hand that held her arm. Ginny knocked and came in with the coffee tray. 'Oh, Helen, are you all right?' she said in a concerned voice. 'Anything I can do?'

Helen shook her head. 'I needed to talk about Humph with Mr Crane, Ginny. You know how I get.'

'She's been in such a state, sir. All we can do is try to help her to get through it.'

'I'm sure you've been a big help, Ginny.'

Ginny poured coffee and then, with a final caring glance, left the room. Helen looked down at her cup. She'd had her coffee black. 'I need this. Too much. I almost took up with the cigarettes again and I've not smoked since I was twenty-five. I've had to make do with coffee and a brandy or three come midnight.'

'Do you want me to leave it for the time being? Come back later when I have more definite news?'

'No,' she said heavily, 'I can cope.' He could sense she was forcing that steely resolve on herself that got her through her evenings at the casino.

'The trouble is, I'm afraid there's more to come. I told you I had a couple of leads. The second one's to do with this man Alphonse Romano.'

It was a sudden rerun of the night at The Fields when she'd scattered ice on the bar when he'd brought up Romano's name. Her cup rattled in its saucer and the liquid lapped over the side. She put down the cup and saucer on a small table but her hand was trembling. '*Alphonse Romano?*' He was certain he heard a note of what sounded like fear in her voice.

'He wants to buy The Fields, Helen, doesn't he?'

'What … what makes you think that?'

'I went to Scarborough on Monday. Do you know what I found? I found that his casino was in a grand old house just like your casino and well out of town. When I went in I thought something had gone wrong in my head because I seemed to be back at The Fields. The restaurant and gaming room are exact replicas of yours, down to the lights, the table layout and the way the croupier girls are dressed, the girls being just as glamorous as yours.'

Her mouth fell open and her eyes widened for the second time. One shock after another, with fear mixed in, he was certain.

'What … what's going on, Frank?' Her tone was one of near-anguish.

'Well, it looked to me as if he felt the way Humph had your own casino couldn't be improved on. Maybe it was a kind of homage to Humph. But there's something else. Romano's casino has a *salon privé*. I managed to catch a glance inside and I found Romano deep in discussion with your Pete Dexter.'

If grief hadn't made her face about as pale as a face could be he felt it would have gone even a shade paler. She gazed at him in silence for some time, hands still trembling. 'Pete,' she said at last. 'What could Pete have been doing there?'

'You've no idea?'

'None.'

Silence fell over the room yet again, the sort of privileged silence that came with expensive houses isolated in their own grounds. Then Crane said, 'Do you not think Romano might be offering Pete a job? Why would Pete be there otherwise? He must know it can be a sacking offence for a casino employee to be found in someone else's casino.'

She didn't speak, looked almost as if she couldn't speak, as if the string of shocks was now affecting her vocal cords. She went on staring at him, the pupils of her eyes rimmed in white.

'Why are you afraid of Romano, Helen?' he said gently. 'Each time his name comes up it seems to give you a scare.'

She got up slowly and crossed to the fireplace, its grate covered by an ornamental wooden screen. There was a looking-glass set above it. She was probably unaware that he could just see the reflection of her face from where he sat. For a couple of seconds she looked very worried. She turned back to him with what seemed a look of distracted anxiety. 'Frank … I'm a woman in what tends to be very much a man's world. Humph looked after business, I concentrated on my restaurant. Alphonse, a few other casino people, they'd meet up at The Fields now and then, have a meal, a drink, swap ideas. They … well they had a lot of respect for Humph and the way he'd built up our place. I can only think Alphonse was so impressed with our set-up that he decided to do exactly the same with his own.'

'To the point of ripping you off staff-wise?'

'I can't believe, I just can't *believe* that Pete, without a word to me, would …' The words dangled. She moved away from the glass and stood before him. 'Alphonse is crowding me,' she told him. 'Yes he does very much want to buy The Fields. He's a nice man, truly, a really nice man, but … well, he's ambitious and he can't let go. That's why I get agitated when you bring his name up. He'd buy the casino tomorrow. But me and Humph, we built it up from nothing, it's all I've really got of Humph in a way, he lived and breathed his casino, it was his life's work.' She sank back down on to the sofa as if suddenly weary, weary of everything, the death, the casino, all the problems the casino seemed to be dumping on her. 'If Alphonse would back off for a year or so, to give me time to *think*, I might eventually want to sell up.'

He nodded slowly. 'But it would be very difficult to manage without Pete, yes? I'm just a layman here but I get the impression Pete's the superior article. He'd be hard to replace, wouldn't he?'

She sighed. 'Near impossible; Humph used to say he was the best he'd ever known. He can spot a card-sharp or a chip-fiddler almost at a single glance. Oh dear, I thought he was happy where he was. I really don't know how I'd carry on without him.'

'Maybe Romano reached the same conclusion.' He thought for a few seconds. 'Look, why not leave it to me to sort Pete out? Like you, I'd be very interested to know what goes on between him and Romano. I can play the honest broker.'

She considered this. 'It should really be me taking it up with him.'

'You're not supposed to know. And he doesn't know I know. I could surprise him.'

'I don't quite understand,' she said. 'Where does surprise come into it? If Pete's leaving he's leaving and I'll have to do the best I can.'

'I'm not sure if Pete knows about Romano's reputation. I don't know if *you* know. It's pretty dubious. My contacts tell me he runs several dodgy scams: drugs, laundering or skimming, maybe even call-girls. And you're right, I think he'd give his eye teeth to get his hands on The Fields. I think he's set his mind on having both jewels in his crown, even maybe to the point of obsession.'

'Oh, Frank!' she burst out, 'you almost seem to be saying he'd do anything to get his hands on it. You can't think, you can't *possibly* think—'

'I'm not certain of anything at the moment, Helen. I'm an ex-CID man and I was trained to keep an open mind until I had hard evidence. I'm simply trying to work through the possibilities of how Humph came to be killed. My gut feeling is that it's down to the drugs people. And yet Romano wants to get his hands on your place so badly that at this stage I can't rule it out that he might somehow be involved.'

'Frank ... Frank ... not *Alphonse*. Humph and me, we got to know him so very well. He's been incredibly kind to me since Humph went. All right, he's pushy in that pleasant way he's got and maybe he does cut a few corners; well, he isn't the only one in this business. I *believe* him when he says that if I don't have The Fields to worry about I'd be all right for money and be able to live an easy life.'

To sit alone in one of her sterile rooms, spending her days in tears, Crane guessed. Her face was a mix of emotions. She called it agitation but he was still certain that it was a kind of fear Romano aroused in her, even though he felt she

had a genuine affection for him. Maybe Romano was the
kind of unnerving presence that could inspire mixed feelings in certain women. Crane had known men of that type.
And maybe he was also the sort of man women responded
to who were in a vulnerable condition,

'Helen, will you let me talk to Pete tonight? I'm impartial
and I think I'll be able to get a straight tale.'

She finally gave a resigned and preoccupied nod. She
gave a decided impression it was all getting to be too much
to cope with. Crane wondered how soon Romano would
cotton on to her low state of mind.

'Jason, guv.'

'Hi, Jase. Go ahead.'

'Manchester. There's no word on the street that anyone's
brooding about any coke deals going arse up. The ripples
always reach the street men in the end, like someone's
thrown a bag of cement in the village pond. Things aren't
just quiet, there's even an atmosphere things are going
pretty well. There's only been one drive-by shooting this
past fortnight, can you believe? And even then the guy
recovered.'

'Must seem like Disneyland.'

'Nice one. I don't suppose it's what you want to hear.'

'Not exactly. I was convinced the gangs had to be
involved.'

'You and me both.'

'Oh well, win some, lose some.'

'Sorry about this but I'll have to charge you fifteen hours, usual rate. That covers staying over at a B and B and the drinks I needed to buy pond life to loosen their tongues.'

'That's all right, Jase, the lady can pay.'

'Is sevenish tomorrow night OK at the Travellers on Duckworth Lane? It'll be a totty called Iris.'

'No prob, Jase,' he said, with a brief abstracted grin, putting down the phone in his small office.

'Jason drawn a blank?' Maggie said, his two hours a day PA.

'Well, it doesn't *seem* to be a gangland killing, even though it has a gangland look.'

'Why *would* a man like Humphrey Todd go up to that driving school place anyway? At night, on his *own*.'

'That's what bugs me. I've had reliable information that the chap who used to deliver the cocaine brought it directly to The Fields. Probably did the business in the back of Todd's car.'

'It would have to have been someone he could really trust, and who had a cast-iron reason to get him up to that funny place.'

'My feelings too, Maggie. Humphrey Todd comes over as having been one streetwise bloke.'

Crane was preparing a simple meal for himself that evening before going up again to The Fields when Terry Jones rang. 'Frank, my oppo across the Pennines rang this PM. This Liam Brent character. There's nothing dodgy about him going missing according to his snout. Brent was East End London by birth and he'd been threatening to go back recently, felt he was getting nowhere in Manchester. He was trusted with negotiating these high-level deals with people like Todd who are into night life in some way. He also moved the actual gear about and always paid on the nail. But he was getting disillusioned. He wanted to be involved in the buying side in Colombia, the logistics of shipping the stuff in. I'm not surprised; your actual barons are netting sixteen, seventeen grand a *day*. And there's us poor buggers sat here! Anyway, my mate's snout reckons he took himself back off to the Smoke.' He chuckled. 'It seems these guys don't go around kissing everyone goodbye and thanking them for the gold watch, they're just away on their toes. Did you know he was a shirt-lifter, by the way?'

'His being gay's the reason I knew he'd gone missing, Terry, but don't ask.'

'You've been at it again, haven't you, talking to blokes who don't talk to bogies. Christ, if I could cut corners like you do.'

Crane sighed. 'Well between them, your mate's snout and my mole, they seem to have knocked a routine gangland killing on the head. I was damn near certain that that was what it was going to turn out to be.'

'Frank, why *did* the bugger go up there? A big wheel in the gambling game. I reckon he was born with a hard nose.'

'You, me, Maggie, we're all humming the same tune.'

*

Crane had a gin and tonic in the bar at The Fields, served to him by one of the waitresses. 'Mrs Todd not in tonight?'

She shook her head. 'She's taking a night off. Are you booked for dinner, sir?'

'No, I'm just going to play a little blackjack.'

'Well, good luck.' She gave him the standard meaningless smile. He walked down from the bar area to the floor. Bishop and Dexter were trawling the tables in their evening wear. Milly was back on duty after throwing her two-evening 'sicky'. She caught sight of Crane as she set the wheel revolving. She didn't give him the wide beam all the women had to perfect but the small trusting smile that went with the delicate looks that lay behind what she'd once called her 'Mask of Cindy' when they'd been at the coast.

Bishop caught his eye next, as Dexter looked to be explaining a rule of the game to one of the gamblers. He came over to him with an anxious smile. '*Hello*, Frank. I was hoping you'd be in soon,' he said, in a low voice. 'I need to talk to you.'

'Can we go in the interview room?'

He looked uneasy. 'I'd sooner not. Pete will only want to know what I've told you. He did the other night. I don't want him to know this, but I'm a lousy liar.'

Crane watched him, wondering if Bishop knew about Dexter's dealings with Romano. 'I could see you later. Your place maybe. Or mine.'

'I'm seeing my old mum after work tonight. She makes me a bit of supper and we have a nice chat. She gets lonely. A day won't make any difference.'

'All right. I'll be up tomorrow night. I need to see Helen. It would be simpler to go to the house but she gets so upset talking about Humph.'

'Oh, I *know*. Heaven knows how she copes, poor thing, with this lot to run.'

'All right. When you're through tomorrow night we'll go somewhere where we can talk. Look, Gerry, a quick word. I'm afraid your friend Liam looks to have gone back to London. That's why you've not been seeing him. I've got it from a source I can trust.'

Bishop sighed. 'Oh dear, I thought it was too good to be true. I'll just have to be philosophical about it. Story of my life.' He looked very hurt.

'Hey, you guys, anything I can share?'

It was Dexter, wearing his usual pleasant smile but managing at the same time to give it a tinge of suspicion.

Crane said, 'Gerry's just been asking if I'd been able to get any further about Humph. The short answer's no, I'm afraid. I understand Helen's not in tonight. It doesn't matter too much as it's you I want to see, Pete.'

Dexter gave him a wary glance. 'Me? I told you every-thing I knew last time.'

'Just one small matter.'

'We're pretty busy—'

'It'll not take long. I've squared it with Helen.'

'We'll go in the interview room. Any problems, Gerry, give me a high five.'

'Oh, I know what to do, Pete,' Bishop said in an aggrieved tone, as if he felt he couldn't be trusted. But Dexter was a driven man and driven men drove others, a trait Romano wouldn't have overlooked.

The two men walked away from the noise of the endlessly clicking balls, the rattle of counters being swept across baize, the mutter of conversation and the clear requests of 'No further bets, please,' to the little room next to the cage. Dexter automatically took up his position at the porthole window, where his flickering eyes began their tireless sweep of the floor. 'How can I help, Frank?'

'Pete, on Monday I became a member of Alphonse Romano's casino, just outside Scarborough. On Tuesday I was able to take a look round.'

Dexter's eyes became fixed for several seconds, the only sign Crane knew he would give of the start he'd just had.

'Why ... did you do that?'

'Mr Romano interests me. He interests me even more now I know his casino is a near-exact replica of The Fields. The only difference I could see was that Romano's place has an actual *salon privé*.'

Dexter's eyes were fixed again and his face had become slightly mottled. 'I ... I never knew that,' he said. 'I did know Mr Romano had always admired what Humph had made of The Fields.'

'But to do his place exactly the same—'

Dexter shrugged. 'I suppose it shows how much he thought of Humph's flair.'

'And you'd no idea?'

'None at all.'

'Well, that's odd, really odd. You must have been walking about with your eyes shut. You see, on Tuesday evening, when a waitress went in the *salon privé* with a tray of drinks I just managed to catch a glimpse of who was inside. There were three blokes: Alphonse Romano, the man who looks as if he could pull a tractor with his teeth and Pete Dexter.'

Dexter's eyes had stopped scanning the floor some time ago. He turned slowly to Crane, the mottling now a flush and his lips quivering. There was a lengthy silence before he managed to speak. 'What ... What's it to you?'

'The answer to that is what's it to *you*? You know you're chancing your job here. Helen knows now, by the way, and she is very, very upset by your disloyalty, on top of all the other shit that's hit her particular fan these past months. She agreed to let me talk to you.'

Dexter watched him again in silence, his fast brain clearly working in overdrive. Finally he said, in a composed tone, 'All right, so you've given me the bad news. I can expect my P45 the next time I see Helen.'

He was back in control. Crane guessed Romano must already have offered him a job. That wasn't surprising, when Dexter was seen as one of the stars of the gaming game.

Crane said, 'Maybe Helen would be prepared to turn a blind eye. You obviously know you'd be very hard to replace. She's thinking things over; I'm acting as honest broker. If she was to forgive and forget would you stay or would you go?'

Dexter shrugged again. 'All right, Romano *has* offered me a job. Manager. Bigger salary, profit share, help with moving house. I'd be in complete charge as Romano doesn't want to be involved in the day-to-day running. He has other irons in the fire.'

'Like the drugs and the laundering and the high-grade call-girls?'

Dexter flushed again. 'I meant his other *clubs*,' he snapped. 'I don't know about anything illegal.'

'Come on, Pete, you weren't born yesterday. If Romano wasn't such a skilled crook he'd have been inside years ago. Don't piss me about.'

Dexter had given up all attempt to monitor the floor. He was very angry, jaws clenched, eyes hard. But he'd spent many years learning to control himself with people who could be very abusive when they'd been caught palming a high-value counter from a colour to a corner. He inhaled deeply, gave Crane his normal friendly smile. 'All right, maybe Romano *does* dabble in one or two things the other side of the law, but casinos and nightclubs, they some-times do get to be run by blokes like Romano. Look, in America, the old-style entertainers: Crosby, Sinatra, Bob Hope, Dean Martin, they'd not have got on so well if they'd not been ready in the early days to play the clubs the gangsters owned. They knew what gangsters *did* but they did their turns, took the money and turned a blind eye. Well, the truth is I don't know all the things Romano gets up to and I don't want to know. All I know is the gambling business and that'll be my only connection with him, running his casino. It's the kind of break that comes up once in a lifetime.'

With reluctance, Crane found himself believing him. The American comparison was a valid one. Dexter had worked in gambling all his life, he knew what could go on, and outside of London Romano's offer had to be the best on the market. He nodded. 'I can see where you're coming from. Just as long as you *do* know the type of man Romano is. I can't quite get it off my mind that Romano's obsession seems to be to own The Fields and the main obstacle to his owning it has recently gone up in a torched car.'

'Christ, you can't think Alphonse had anything to do with *that?*'

Crane sighed. 'To be honest, no. Not his style, so I've been told. I'm beginning to accept that it's just a coincidence. I'm still inclined to think the killing was a drugs-related contract. You did know Humph was selling the nose-candy to the big rollers?'

With a faintly sheepish grin, Dexter nodded.

'You should have told the police *or* me, but we'll let that pass. You were thinking of the club's reputation, I know.'

'That's the truth.'

'Well, I think that's it, Pete. You've been straight with me and I appreciate it. I'll be speaking to Helen tomorrow night. I'll give her the gist of what you've told me. She'll want to talk to you about it, maybe up Romano's offer.'

'I'm sorry you've not got anywhere ... about Humph.'

Crane shrugged. 'You know what Churchill used to say. KBO – keep buggering on. I do a lot of that in my line of work.'

'Frank, I don't want to seem disloyal to Helen. She's always treated me well. It's just that the way things are going I reckon I'll be working for Romano sooner or later whether I stay or go.'

'I daresay you're right.' He smiled. 'But if you do decide to sup with the devil make sure you've got plenty of long spoons in your cutlery drawer.'

'That you, Pete?'

'Yes, Alphonse.'

'Got rid of the gumshoe yet?'

'Afraid not. He nailed me earlier this evening. He said he'd been over to Scarborough to check your casino out.'

Romano was silent for a few seconds. 'Did he now? Did he say why?'

'He just seems to be running a check on everyone who was involved with Humph. I think he was a bit suspicious that you've been wanting to buy The Fields and Humph got himself killed.'

Romano fell silent again. 'Dear me,' he said, 'is he still thinking that way, do you think?'

'No. He accepts it was a coincidence. He's pretty sure he got across the drugs people in some way.'

'Everyone with half a brain knew that all along, Pete. The drugs people don't give you two chances and they don't fuck around, not with ten kilos of that stuff costing upwards of two hundred grand. That's why they did a spectacular on Humph, God rest him, to make sure no one else is thinking of pulling the same stunt.'

'Just by the way, Alphonse, Crane saw me at your place. He caught a glimpse of me with you and Billy when Sharon pushed the door open of the *salon privé* to bring the drinks in.'

'The guy seems to have eyes in his arse, I'll give him that. What did you tell him?'

'The truth. That you'd offered me a job and I was thinking about it.'

'And that was it?'

'No. He hinted you did a bit of coke and one or two things like that. I told him I knew nothing, I'd just be there to run Romano's.'

'Very wise, Pete. You're a good friend and I've never pretended with you about the coke and one or two other little things I'd sooner the law didn't know about. Or the Revenue. But I'm getting seriously worried now with this guy poking about. It's not that I don't want poor Humph's killer found, though I don't honestly think there's much chance of that, but this guy seems pretty sharp and he might, just might, get to know a bit too much about my little sidelines. I told Helen not to do it, hire a PI, said it would only give her more grief. When's he going to butt out, Pete?'

'I don't give it much longer. He's seeing her tomorrow night at The Fields and he's got sod all to tell her. I can't see her keeping him on, she's not the type to throw money away. I daresay he'll want to spin it out though, it must be a nice little earner.'

'That bugs me too. Maybe I'll have a word with her, try

and persuade her to let him go before he wastes any more of her money. Well done, Pete, I'm relying on you to keep me up to speed.'

EIGHT

He'd taken her to the beer garden of the Fox and Grapes again. He liked her company, didn't want her to feel he was simply using her to help with the case. He liked seeing her in non-casino mode with her hair loosely brushed and that slightly ethereal look she had without the heavy make-up, a look that was enhanced by the faint melancholy that shadowed her features when she wasn't on duty. She was dressed in her good casual clothes of jeans, roll-neck and woollen jacket against the still cool spring weather.

He said, 'I'll be seeing Helen tonight. I think I'll tell her she can keep me on if she feels she must, but I can't honestly see anywhere else to go.'

'Your work must be very frustrating.'

'You live with it. I'm also seeing Gerry. He says he needs to talk to me. He might just have something to say that could be of use.'

He saw the faintest touch of colour in her cheeks. 'I'd not put too much faith in what Gerry says. He can be a bit of a washerwoman.'

The waitress came out with their lunch order, a tuna salad for Milly, a beef sandwich in French bread for Crane. When she'd laid out the plates and the cutlery and a glass of rosé for Milly, and left, Crane said, 'Didn't you tell me a little while ago that part of Gerry's value to the casino was the way he looked after the girls? They felt they could tell him things that went no further. Well, he just might be able to tell me something about Humph that would help.'

Her colour had deepened and she sat in silence, probably remembering that she *had* told Crane that Bishop had a feel for the gossip and knew how to be discreet. It suddenly struck him that maybe the casino girl herself could tell him something about Todd that might be useful. He was certain she'd been involved with him even though she'd never admitted it. Perhaps a sense of tact had held him back; she had after all given him a lot of help in other ways, even if nothing much had come of it. It was totally impossible to imagine that this fine young woman could be remotely connected to any chain of events that could have led to Todd's death, but she might know something, even unwittingly, that could give him another possible lead.

'Maybe,' Crane said slowly, 'maybe Gerry might be going to tell me something about *your* involvement with Humph, Milly.'

The flush rapidly deepened. '*My* involvement! What can you *mean*, Frank?'

'I mean that I'm certain you've had a double helping of sadness dumped on you, not just Sophie's death but Humph's too.'

She sat in silence, her food and wine untouched. She began to look very troubled. Then she said, 'What if I was involved with him? It makes absolutely no difference to your case, unless you think *I* went up to the driving-school place with gallons of petrol.'

'Milly,' he said gently, 'you know I couldn't possibly think anything like that. Your private life's your own. The only reason I bring it up is that you just might have heard something from Humph that means nothing to you but just might mean something to me. I really didn't mean to upset you.'

She fell silent once more, against the cheerful sounds of talk and laughter from people in sight of weekend freedom. Her lips moved, more than once, almost as if she was on the point of telling him something she wished she *could* get off her mind. At the end of the long silence, she said, 'You're right, I was seeing Humph. You can't believe how attractive to women he was, how charismatic. It was overwhelming. Yes, I did go to work at the casino because of him. It was when I went there for a meal that time. Someone's birthday. Just the restaurant, not the gambling. Humph had this thing of going to every table, making sure people were enjoying their meal and hoping to see you again if it was your first visit, all that.

'Just as we were leaving, Humph asked me if I'd spare him a moment. He asked very discreetly if I'd be interested in casino work, I was just the type they were always on the look-out for. He said if I ever wanted to talk it over to give him a ring ... he gave me his card. He said that whatever I was earning he'd improve on it.

'I … I took the job. It was well-paid and good tips on top. But … well … it was Humph. I could tell he fancied me, and …'

The words dangled. Crane nodded, gave her an understanding smile. He wasn't sure he was getting the exact truth. He couldn't quite believe an intelligent middle-class girl like her would throw up a job with good prospects for an insecure job with unsocial hours in a casino because she'd fallen for the owner, even if he did come over like Brad Pitt. 'All right, Milly, I understand. But you must have had an idea Humph had a bit of a reputation with the ladies. It seems to have been known to quite a few people except Helen.'

She shook her head. 'I didn't, truly. I thought it was just me and that his marriage was a sham. I honestly didn't get much involved in the casino gossip. I knew he was *good* with women, obviously. I thought it was simply business, to lure them to the tables.'

'You never had the slightest hint from Humph he might be in any sort of trouble? Nothing at all?'

She shook her head again. She was still very uneasy. 'He seemed to have the sort of mind where you can put your business worries and so on to one side. He was always cheerful when he was with me, never gave any impression anything was bugging him.'

Crane ate some of his sandwich. Milly began to pick at her salad without much appetite. She put down her fork, sipped a little of the rosé. Then she put a hand over his. 'I'm sorry, Frank, there *is* more. I'd rather not tell you till you've finished the case … or dropped it. It's nothing to do with

Humph's death, not in the slightest way, and it won't make any difference to anything when I *do* tell you.'

He watched her. 'If it's something you've not told anyone about it might ease your mind to share it. You know you can trust me.'

She nodded unhappily. 'I could trust you with my life. I'll give you the full story when you're out of the case. Believe me, Frank, when you do hear it you'll see what a total irrelevance it is to what happened to Humph.'

He didn't push it, knew it would be pointless. It was a secret he couldn't begin to guess at; he'd just have to take her word for it that it had no bearing on the case. He was sure she was right but he'd very much liked to have known all the same.

'I wish I could bring myself to tell you, Frank, it really would ease my mind. I will later, when things get back to normal,' she said sadly. 'If they ever do.'

The restaurant was very quiet at this late hour. Helen sat behind a desk in a little room that adjoined the kitchen.

'Take a seat, Frank,' she said, when one of the waitresses showed him in. 'Can we get you anything ... G and T? Coffee?'

'Nothing just now, Helen, thanks.'

'This is the restaurant back office.' A CDU stood to one side on her desk, neatly annotated box files lined wall shelves. 'Bills,' she told him, 'credit-card dockets, Health and Safety. Health and Safety could just about do with its own shelf these days.'

'And this is all waiting for you when you've finished your front of house?'

'Tell me about it.' She rolled her eyes, smiled. 'But this is the entertainment business. You saw Pete, I suppose. How did he take it?'

He told her how it had gone. 'I think he was genuinely sorry that you had to hear it the way you did and thought he was being disloyal. He just felt he had to see what was on the table with Romano's offer. He's an ambitious young man. He pointed out, rightly I suppose, that Romano's job will be one of the best outside London.'

'Why ... why is Alphonse doing this to me? He must know how hard I'll find it to replace Pete.'

'I think we both know the answer to that. With Humph gone and Pete gone you'll find it near impossible to run The Fields.'

'Oh dear, I just don't want to sell up, at least not for a couple of years. I know Alphonse would give me a fair price but, quite apart from anything else, he'll give me a better one the longer I hold out.'

Crane had to admire the way she never let her endless grief about Todd interfere with her hard-headed business sense.

'What do you think, Frank? Have you any idea what might make Pete stay?'

Crane thought about this and the two discussions he'd had with Dexter.

'Well,' he said, 'I don't know if Humph ever talked this over with you, but he once told Pete that you both might want to retire in a few years and not sell up but let Pete run

The Fields on a profit-share basis. That would put him in charge and that seems to be the sort of career step he wants. It could be that he'd prefer to stay in this area too. Maybe you could think of something on those lines?'

She watched him in silence as she considered this. 'You know, that *might* do the trick. I could become, say, a sleeping partner, though I'd still want to run the restaurant for a few years, and Pete could take control of everything else. Do you think that might hold him?'

'I don't know. Romano has quite a little empire apparently: clubs, one or two city casinos. He could be dangling a much bigger carrot altogether. It's worth a try, though.'

She nodded. 'And if one day I offered *Pete* the chance to buy me out if he could raise the backing...?'

'That could be the clincher.'

But Crane suspected that whatever inducement she threw in that might encourage Dexter to stay, sooner or later, as Dexter himself had said, whatever he did he'd still end up working for Romano.

She smiled. 'I engaged you as a PI, Frank. I really shouldn't be getting you to wear a personnel hat as well. But I really am very grateful for your help and advice.'

He also smiled. 'That's all right, Helen. I needed to clear things up with Pete anyway, about finding him in such close contact with Romano. I had to make sure there was nothing sinister going on, especially when I'd found Romano's place to be an exact match with The Fields.'

She wasn't putting ice in a glass this time or holding a cup of coffee, but her hands were trembling just as they'd done then. She caught his eyes on them and put them out of sight below the top of her desk. She said uneasily, 'Oh, I'm … I'm sure with Alphonse it was just a question of imitation being the sincerest form of flattery. And wanting to poach Pete … Well, he is a businessman, I suppose, though I am rather hurt that he'd see Pete behind my back.'

She'd said it was agitation, the way she reacted whenever he talked about Romano, the pressure he kept putting on her to sell out to him, but Crane was still convinced there was something about the man that frightened her, as if he really did have some kind of hold over her.

'Well, Romano does seem to be wanting to rush things with you, Helen, and offering Pete the top position here might be the answer.'

'I'll … I'll get Pete in now,' she said. 'It's not a situation I can afford to let drift. Thanks again, Frank.'

He got up. 'Just one other thing, Helen. I need to ask you if you want to keep me on. Frankly, I'm pretty sure Humph's death is somehow connected to the drugs people, but I'd be lying if I said I thought I could ever prove it.'

'No, no,' she said quickly, 'I can't let you go just yet. I want you to stay another week at least. Please don't give in. I'm so desperate to know for certain, if ever possible….'

Out on the floor, when Crane saw Dexter heading towards the restaurant area, he said to Bishop, 'When do you get through, Gerry?'

'About three-quarters of an hour. Could you give me a lift, Frank? My wheels are in for repair to something called a half-shaft, whatever that might be. It'll save the firm a taxi. My flat's down Cunliffe Road, if that isn't too far out of your way.'

'No problem. I'll see you in the car park.'

'Thanks ever so.'

Crane changed a couple of tenners at Milly's table and played his usual modest game to while away the time, betting on colours and columns, then occasionally throwing caution to the wind and indulging himself with a corner or a double street. Milly, apart from the standard wide smile of welcome, gave no indication she knew him beyond the brief, intimate, almost subliminal smiles she gave him now and then when people were laying their new bets. Since their lunch at the Fox he'd wondered a number of times exactly what could have gone on between her and Todd she couldn't yet bring herself to tell him.

Gerry waited in the car park. He'd changed from his evening clothes into a brushed fabric jacket and cotton twill slacks that looked so fashionably up to the minute that, like his hair care, it was unlikely they'd have been available in Bradford. They walked to Crane's car.

'Oh, is this yours, Frank! So shiny and new-looking.'

'It's a year old. I keep it valeted. Some of the people I work for, it wouldn't be a good idea to roll up in a scruffy old model. And I spend so much time in it I like to be comfortable.'

'Oh, I'd *love* a nice car. I only ever seem able to run to second-hand ones with at least forty on the clock. I keep telling my old mum, "One day, Mummy, I'll be able to run to a brand-new one and when that day comes I'll take you up to the Devonshire Arms for your Sunday lunch".'

'Your mum didn't remarry?'

'She'd had enough with first one. Never out of the pub and shouting the odds when he was. She's just got me. I'd live with her but, well, she'd not be able to get it together, me taking guys home instead of gals. She has a little cottage in Daisy Hill and I pop in two or three times a week, keep an eye on her, help her with the gas bills and so forth. I suppose this lovely motor has ABS and air conditioning and a CD player and an immobilizer and goes peep-peep if you forget to turn off the lights.'

Crane grinned. 'Goes bananas if you forget to fasten your seat belt and move more than a foot.'

'Humph would sometimes send me on errands in his gorgeous Merc. Lovely bronze colour. Top of the range, even had a little telly for folk in the back. Driving it was like floating on air.'

Crane, hand on door, hesitated. He was intensely proprietorial with his cars, they were like a second home, but he could see that Gerry was the type of man who'd treat decent wheels with the respect they deserved. 'Look,' he said, 'if you'd care to drive, Gerry, be my guest.'

'Oh, Frank, *could* I? Are you sure you'd not mind? I'd be very, very careful.'

'I'm sure. If Humph could trust you with his top of the range Merc I think I can trust you with my middle of the range Renault.'

He tossed Bishop the keys. About to get in on the passenger side, he had another thought. 'Look, just give me five minutes, Gerry, I'll see if I can catch Helen before she leaves.'

'Okey-dokey. I'll bring the car round to the front while you're gone.'

Crane hurried back to the casino, curious to see if his personnel work had paid off and Helen had persuaded Dexter to stay on board. If it had paid off he'd at least have provided her with something positive for the money she was paying him. When he reached the reception area, she was just walking across it, wearing a light raincoat.

'Ah, Helen,' he said, 'glad I've caught you. Just wondered how you got on with Pete.'

The second she began to speak there was a sudden explosion, so close and so massive it could have been a gas-main blowing up.

NINE

Shocked and speechless, they both rushed out to the car park. Crane's car was a roaring ball of flame.

'Frank, what's happened!' she screamed, both hands to the sides of her face. 'What's *happened*!'

Other people were now scurrying from the casino: the last handful of gamblers, members of staff. 'Keep back!' Crane, shouted. 'Keep well back, all of you. There could be another explosion.'

'Frank, what's *happened*!'

But he was already keying the police on his mobile. 'My name's Frank Crane. I'm speaking from The Fields casino at the top of Thornton Road. My car's been blown up in the car park. I think it was a deliberate murder attempt. There was a man inside who'll now be dead.'

The thin crowd stood just outside the casino, faces frozen in shock and lit by the glare of the roaring flames as if they were at a bonfire.

Dexter shouted, 'Whose, car is it, Frank? Any idea?'

'It was my Renault and Gerry was in it.'

'God almighty! What was he doing in *your* car?'

But Crane was now keying Terry Jones's home number. 'Terry, I've rung the station but you need to know this. My car's just been blown up at The Fields casino. There was someone inside it so we'll need SOCOs.'

'Christ, where were *you*? No, tell me later. I'm on my way. I'll get Ted along too.'

'Frank, why has your car been blown *up*?' Helen cried.

'Because someone was certain I'd be in it.'

The croupier girls stood near Dexter in a shocked huddle, shaking and whispering to one another with trembling lips. Milly stood a little apart, open-mouthed, gazing from the blazing vehicle to Crane and back, as if barely able to believe he was still alive.

'Helen,' Crane said firmly, 'will you and Pete get these people back inside? No one to leave till the police have spoken to them. Give them drinks, coffee, whatever ...'

Crane stayed outside. Fortunately his car stood isolated from the sprinkling of others; none of them appeared to be damaged. Very soon a fire engine drew in off the road, followed by a warbling ambulance and a panda. Behind them at intervals came unmarked cars, Jones in one, Benson in another, men in a third who would probably have the forensic skills.

'What in hell's going on, Frank?' Jones called, even before he was out of his car.

'I should have been in that car, Terry.' He briefly explained how it was Bishop had been the one to turn the key in the ignition that had detonated the explosives that must have been attached to the underside of the car some-time during the evening.

'Who could have *done* it, Frank?'

'I don't know. I've not had time to think about it.'

'Something to do with Todd buying it?'

'What else?'

'Not another of those sodding gangland carry-ons!'

The firemen and the paramedics were in a huddle with the uniformed police and the men in plain clothes. The car fire was beginning to die down and Crane guessed that the police would be concerned that a deluge of foam might destroy any possible forensic evidence. It was obvious that all that was left of Bishop would be cinders.

'It's an open and shut case, Terry,' Crane said heavily. 'Only you'll be opening and shutting an empty file. Whoever did this will be playing poker with five guys who'll say he was there all night, in the unlikely event you ever get to feel collars. You've got another Humph Todd show on your hands.'

'The earache we'll get from the councillors,' Jones said grimly. 'Two so close together, both connected to this place. They'll be asking are we going the same way as Manchester? Well, let's get inside and me and the lads can start talking to people.'

'I've told Helen not to let anyone go.'

Jones sighed. 'It'll not make a fart's worth of difference whether they stay or go. How are you holding up, old son, to say you've just missed being blown to bits?'

'All that's pumping round my system is pure adrenaline.'

Jones nodded. He was police and Crane had once been police and they had both had their share of physical danger. You accepted that it could be a dangerous job and that the adrenaline would see you through. It was the downside that followed that you had to be prepared for. Jones knew it was going to hit him like clinical depression when it really hit him that he was only alive by pure chance.

The police worked steadily on, taking names and addresses, asking where people had been when the car exploded and had they seen anyone acting suspiciously in the car park at any time during the evening. People were then allowed to go home. Crane stood to one side, sipping brandy from a tumbler he held with a hand he couldn't now stop trembling. Milly caught his eye as she was released from questioning. 'Frank, I don t know what to *say*. It's frightful, *frightful*! How will you get home?'

'Inspector Jones ... he'll drop me off.'

Even the heavy make-up couldn't conceal her pallor. She was very frightened. She had to hold a mug of coffee in both hands to get it to her quivering lips. 'Drop ... drop you off at *home*?

'Where else, Milly?'

'Don't ... don't you think ... if that blown-up car was meant for you, and whoever did it finds you're still alive, won't you still be in danger if you do go to your own house?'

The kid had it right. He felt as if his brain had been disarranged and wouldn't come together to function in the normal way. He was now a marked man, unable to go safely to his house in case a trained killer came to put right the job he'd botched the first time. 'You're right. I'm not thinking straight.'

'How could you be? Do you … shall I take you to my place?'

'That's going to put *you* in danger.'

'I'll take a chance. To be honest, I'd like you around.'

He nodded. 'I could do with the company myself. Thanks, Milly.'

'I'll wait for you in reception.'

He watched her walk slowly off, a long cardigan over her casino clothes. She had to be wondering when it was all going to end: Humphrey Todd in a torched car, Gerry Bishop in a blown-up car, her sister raped and left to drown in a Jacuzzi.

He went to sit with Jones in the bar area. He tried to tell him everything he'd done on the case, but his brain still had that scattered feel and he kept vaguely repeating himself and backtracking. Jones put a hand on his arm. 'Save it for tomorrow, Frank, when you've had a night's sleep. Will you come down to the station then and I'll take a full official statement?'

Crane felt almost weak now with reaction. 'I'm sorry, Terry, I'm not making much sense.'

'Finish your drink and I'll wrap up here. I can put you up at my place. That might be best, the way things are.'

Jones too had picked up on the danger that going back to his own house might put him in. 'It's all right, Terry. Milly, the young woman who's been my contact here, she's offered me a room at her place.'

'That's fine, but take care.'

He gave a small wry grin. Crane had always had an ability to pull the totty. Jones, slightly envious, had never been able to understand why, as he hadn't much in the way of looks or charm-school talk. 'I might have to think of putting your place under obbo.'

'It would be a waste of time,' Crane said. 'Maybe they'll think me bricking it is as good as being killed, for getting me off the case....'

'Frank, what can it all *mean?*' Milly said, as she drove her small Citroën down the near-deserted Thornton Road.

'They must have thought I know too much. About Humph's killer. When all I really know is damn all.'

'Poor *Gerry*. Oh, it's *ghastly*. Such a nice chap, wouldn't harm a fly.'

Crane wondered how he was ever going to learn to live with it, that a decent, good-hearted gay had been pointlessly robbed of his life in his place.

'Why did he have your car keys?'

'He was mad about decent cars; he could only afford second-hand ones. We were going back to his place, so he could tell me what he must have thought might help with the case. I told him he could drive if he'd like to.'

Crane began to tremble uncontrollably again. 'We were within minutes of us both being killed. There was something I wanted to ask Helen before she left. I told him to hang on, I'd be right back. He said he'd bring the car round to the front. And it was quite *unnecessary*, me going back, that is what I can't get off my mind, it wasn't anything that couldn't have waited. It wasn't even anything to do with the case. But I go, that poor devil gets blown to pieces.'

'You mustn't blame yourself. Believe me I know what I'm talking about here.' She took a hand briefly from the wheel and put it over one of his. 'How were you to *know*? How could you possibly have known?'

But Crane was in free fall from the adrenaline surge that had helped him to cope so rapidly and effectively with the car explosion. He couldn't get Bishop's appalling death off his mind, that likeable man with his elegant clothes and careful grooming, and the simple pleasure he took in being allowed to drive the Renault, with its anti-lock braking system and its air conditioning and the insistent warnings it would give you if you forgot to turn off the lights. Crane had once been in danger from a man with a knife, but if that incident had led to his death it would have been his own death, not one he could have avoided by having someone else in his place.

Milly angled off Thornton Road to take the series of minor roads that would take them across to her house in Highgate. 'So … you never found out what it was Gerry wanted to tell you?'

'He wanted to tell me in private, away from the casino,' he said heavily.

'I wonder what it could have been?'

His brain still had the scrambled feel the triple shock had induced: the exploding car, Bishop's death, and the dead man that he himself should have been. It was only later that he wondered if he might have heard a note of relief in her voice that he'd not known, nor would ever know, what it had been that Bishop was anxious to tell him.

The quiet normality of Milly's house helped him a little after the turmoil at The Fields. There were modern sofas that angled a corner of the living room, a gas log fire which she lit, a flat-screen television, abstract-patterned curtains, framed prints of paintings by Braque. He slumped wearily on to one of the sofas, hands still shaking, depression seeming to seep over his mind as unstoppably as darkness filtering across an evening sky.

'Drink?'

'Brandy if you've got it.'

She went off to the kitchen and came back with a tumbler half-full of the strong spirit. She had a small gin. She put the tray with the drinks on a small table, took hold of one of his quivering hands, heavy eyes on his. It was too heavy a burden for one so young, all the deaths, Crane a near-miss, and not even a parent to turn to for comfort. Even the death of a daughter, it seemed, however deeply they felt it, wasn't allowed to interfere for very long with their ambitious lives.

'He was saving up for a brand-new car,' he said, in a low voice. 'He wanted one gleaming new from the show room. Humph would let him drive his Mercedes now and then. He just loved cars. Be my guest, I told him, be my guest to find what's left of yourself in a body bag. If there *is* anything left.'

'You must stop this. How could you possibly be to blame?'

'If I'd not gone to see Helen—'

'Then you'd *both* be dead. What good would that be?'

'He's got an old mum. He's all she's got. He looked after her. Always calling in, helping with the bills.'

She fell silent, letting him talk on. His words, to his own ears, seemed to come from a distance. 'Why Gerry?' he couldn't stop himself repeating. 'He was just trying to help me, about Humph. I think he loved Humph like a father. His own cleared off when he was just a baby.'

She still held his hand. Maybe she thought it would be therapeutic to let him endlessly ramble. From inside his tunnel of depression he wished to God it could be therapeutic.

When he'd lapsed into silence, she said, 'Frank, I know where you are, I really do. When Sophie died … I'd never known what depression was. The doctor gave me a sick note. I just sat at home. I felt I couldn't do the smallest job in the house. I hardly ate, hardly even washed or cleaned my teeth. I didn't know how I could live without her.

'Then I began to blame myself, just as you're doing. Sophie was fun-loving, a bit giddy, not as streetwise as me. I felt I should have kept a closer eye on her.

'It took me a long time to come round,' she went on with a faint smile, 'and a lot too much gin. I felt she'd torn out part of my soul and taken it with her. But I knew I couldn't go on like that. I forced myself back to work. It was the very worst time of my life. I don't think I'll ever grieve for anyone the way I grieved for her. So you see, I know all about depression.'

He nodded, drained his glass. His mental upheaval didn't begin to compare with the one she'd had to go through, but there was kindness in the comparison. Her words had brought him comfort. 'Thanks, Milly. I'll not forget this.'

'Come on,' she said, 'let's get some sleep. You'll see things in a different light in the morning. And you *must* stop blaming yourself.'

She led him upstairs, pointed to a bedroom. 'The bed's made up. It was Sophie's room.' She hesitated. 'Or … you can come with me to my room.'

'I'd like that….'

He lived a solitary life and it suited him, but tonight he didn't want to be alone. He wanted to be held. He sensed the same longing in her.

'This time you'll be caught without pyjamas.'

'That's all right, I've got my overnight bag …' He broke off. The rubble of his car now included the rubble of his overnight bag. He forced a wry smile. 'You're right, this time it'll be me in the buff.'

'I'm not wanting sex, Frank.'

'I know.'

'I'm not wanting to poach you from your partner.'

'I know that too. She's not my partner. She's just a close friend I sometimes sleep with.'

'Can I be a close friend too?'

'I'd say you already were.'

But in the silent darkness of her bed, when they were two people trying to ease the pain of their traumas in the warmth and closeness of their bodies, she whispered, 'You don't really want sex, do you, with everything that's happened?'

'I thought I didn't.'

'I thought I didn't last Monday. And then I did. I felt I was coming back into the real world.'

So they made love, made love almost with a kind of desperation. Maybe Milly still sought the kind of normality other women took for granted: boyfriends, nights out, girlfriends to go shopping with, holidays in the sun. With Crane it was like an overwhelming surge of relief, a resounding confirmation that the life force still ran through him, that he was still triumphantly alive when he should have been dead.

'It's Pete, Alphonse. Sorry it's so late.'

'That's OK, Pete, how are things?'

'Not good. Frank Crane, the PI, his car's been blown up.'

'Dear God, Pete, what's this you're telling me?'

'It gets worse. Crane wasn't *in* his car. It was Gerry Bishop. Crane had lent him the car for some reason.'

'Pete … Pete. That nice young gay got killed in his *place*! What in hell's going on?'

'It's *got* to be the drugs people. That's the sort of thing they *do*. Crane must have found out too much.'

'He's one clever guy at finding things out. When did it go up, this car?'

'Late last night. Crane had spent some time with Helen. He was trying to broker a deal between me and her so I'd stay on at The Fields. She wants me to stay on as manager. She'd not sell out but give me a profit share.'

'Sounds a good deal, son.'

'I said I'd think about it, but I'd prefer to work for you.'

'You'll have better prospects with me and sooner or later I'm sure I'll persuade Helen to sell me the casino. But this Crane thing, Pete. I'm sure you're right, it's got to be the Manchester connection, it's too similar to how poor Humph went. Crane's been one very lucky guy. He must have had his rosary in his pocket.'

'I can't see him carrying on, Alphonse. Nothing's worth getting yourself killed for.'

'Too right. Well, I'm sorry about Gerry, I really am, but I have to say if it stops Crane poking around in things that don't concern him there is some kind of a plus.'

'I wish to God Helen had never set him on. It's just made things worse.'

'I did tell her it wouldn't be a good idea, Pete....'

T E N

'I don't do much in the way of breakfast, but there's toast, cornflakes, fruit.'

'I don't do breakfast at all. Just coffee, if you have it, strong, black, just the one sugar.'

'It'll have to be instant.'

'Home from home.'

'What will you do? About going home?'

'Give it a miss for a couple of days. I need time to think things out.'

'Do you want to stay here?'

'I really don't want to put you in any danger.'

'I'll take the chance. No one will know you're with me.'

'I doubt anyone will go for me again. When they know I'm still alive they'll figure the shock they've handed me will be as good as taking me out. They just want me off the case. Well, much as I dislike packing a case in I'm not prepared to handle danger on this scale.'

Milly said, 'My gran lived to a very good age. Then she became ill and knew she wasn't going to get better. She hated the idea of dying. "You see, dear," she said to me, "one gets so addicted to life." They're the sort of words you don't forget.'

'I couldn't have put it better, after last night.'

She smiled up at him. 'It looks as if we're both in packing in mode. I've decided I'm not going back to work at the casino. I only went there because of Humph, only stayed on to see if the police, or you, tracked down who killed him.'

'You may not be the only one deciding to leave. And it could be a while before the punters start coming back. I doubt they'll be too keen on exploding cars in casino car parks. It'll be a while before the police let the wreckage be moved. The forensic people will be sifting through every ounce of it. People expert in blowing cars apart sometimes leave a kind of footprint. They tend to attach the explosives and wire them up to the ignition in a certain way that can provide clues.' He sighed. 'Though I doubt it will get them anywhere. Men who can wire up a car quickly and effectively usually have similar expertise about vanishing into thin air.'

She put down his coffee on the little kitchen table. 'What will you do now?'

'Work. Like you, it's my answer to most things.'

He thought he'd not sleep, but he had, heavily, with what had to have been a profound urge for a release from the tragic events of last night, for a chance for his brain to reformat itself into its normal operating mode. He'd awoken still in a state of depression about Bishop, but thinking more or less rationally. The kid was right, he couldn't go on blaming himself for Bishop's death, for not being in the car to die himself as intended. Perhaps that was where the real guilt lay, that his own addiction to life could only make him so intensely relieved and glad that he'd been the one left standing.

These had been difficult thoughts to carry around, and this morning he felt more able to pack them into that near-sealable corner of his mind where the other baggage of his life was stored, never forgotten but rarely re-examined: the loss of his successful police career, the making do with PI work, the loss of the only woman he'd ever wanted to marry.

Milly drove him to the Renault show room at the city end of Thornton Road, where he hired a Laguna. He'd have to lock horns with the insurers about a replacement vehicle. He wasn't sure how the deliberate destruction of his vehicle would be treated, but he couldn't at this stage find the will to start the ball rolling, with all the paperwork and phone calls that would be involved. Perhaps he could get Maggie to do it. The simple answer was to order a new car and hope the insurance pay-out would cover two-thirds of it. He was in a position these days to be able to afford to do that. But not today.

He then drove to his house, parked carefully some distance away to ensure it wasn't receiving any undue attention, then went in and changed his shirt and underwear and packed a case with other clothes and the sorts of things he kept in the car to while away the time while on obbo: music CDs, CDs of talking books. There was no client data lost in the explosion, he kept that either in his memory, in an inside pocket, or stored on Maggie's computer. He then drove to his modest office in the Old Quarter.

'You'll be reading about a car being blown up at The Fields casino any time now, Maggie. Well, you heard it here first. It was mine.' As her mouth fell open, he went on, 'You'll be pleased to know I wasn't in it. To prove it I'm here.'

He gave her the details briefly, as she sat in a stunned silence. 'I was never happy about you taking that case, Frank,' she said, when he'd finished. 'Not with the way Humphrey Todd was killed. It had gangsters written all over it.'

'I was never too happy myself. I did try to talk Helen Todd out of it, but she was desperate to know who'd do a thing like that to Humph. I felt sorry for her.'

She didn't speak for some time. She shook her head. 'That poor young man. How did whoever did that to your car know you'd be at the casino last night?'

'I can see you've not forgotten the sort of stuff you used to type up when you were a PA in the force. That was the first thing I asked myself when I began to think straight.'

From his office he went to the central police station to see Terry Jones. He gave him the details clearly and consecutively this time of everything he'd done in the Todd case. Jones made rapid and detailed notes. 'All right, Frank, that's fine. I wish everyone could be so concise. I won't pretend that any of this is going to take us anywhere. The forensics might come up with something and then again the Chancellor might drop the top rate to twenty pence. Are you sure you're OK this morning?' He smiled faintly. 'I could arrange counselling to talk you through the trauma.'

Crane also smiled. 'A couple of stiff brandies did the trick, as it turned out.'

Together with a night being comforted by the little croupier totty, Jones thought wistfully. 'I've got that Dexter bloke coming in this afternoon. He obviously just about runs the place with Todd gone. We spent a good while with him when Todd got seen to, but got sod all out of him worth spit, nothing about Todd being into drugs, for example, which he had to have known and should have let on about. Well, this is the second car to go up in smoke to do with that bloody casino and I'm not minded to give him too easy a ride this afternoon. You don't think *he* could have known what Bishop was going to tell you?'

Crane shook his head. 'That's why Gerry wanted to see me well away from the casino. He didn't *want* Dexter to know.'

Jones sighed. 'Could have been a valuable lead. If Bishop didn't want Dexter to know could that mean Dexter might somehow have been implicated in the Todd carry-on?'

'I don't honestly think so. The chap's streetwise, no question, but I get the impression he's pretty straight. But I woke up this morning asking myself who *knew* I'd be at The Fields last night. Well, two people knew for certain: Bishop and Dexter. Gerry's gone now, poor sod, and I'm pretty certain he'd have no reason to pass it on. But Dexter, well he just *could* have passed it on, passed it on to Alphonse Romano, a bloke he's considering going to work for.'

'Why would he tell Romano?'

Crane shrugged. 'Maybe he told Romano things. About me checking out Romano's place, say, and then telling Dexter I'd felt I had to tell Helen I'd caught him in bed with Romano.'

Jones watched him in silence for a short time. 'You weren't making too much sense last night and I'm not surprised. But what you told *me* about Romano had me giving a bell to the Scarborough police this morning. The bugger has no form but they know damn fine he's a shady sod. He's not a man who'd like to hear about a PI keeping an eye on him.'

'And maybe he encouraged Pete to tell him exactly what I was up to.'

'What are we saying here, Frank?'

'I'm still not sure. Those two blokes I spoke to, the part-time inspectors at The Fields: Salter and Brogan. It was they who filled me in on Romano being bad news. They've been in the gambling game all their lives and they had the inside track on him. They knew he was in the scams but they were pretty sure he wasn't a man who settled disputes by killing people. That's how I tended to see it too. I'd pinned down the Romano–Todd connection, but I couldn't see him killing Todd. Or me either, very nearly.'

Jones watched him in another silence. He was a strong heavy man who seemed to wear a permanent expression of cynical fatigue in the endless battle against the ever-growing new kinds of crime that were flourishing in the high-tech twenty-first century. 'This helps me. I'll press

Dexter hard about Romano, try and winkle out whether he did speak to him the night you told *him* you'd be at The Fields last night. If I throw it at him he might react.'

Crane sighed. 'Probably be another dead end, Terry. These car murders, they've got drug-land written all over them. I just feel I'm missing something.'

Jones shrugged. 'On the other hand, Romano might not be a man who kills people, but he could know a man who does.'

Crane returned to the type of work that took up the bulk of his time: divorce problems, lifestyle checks, various kinds of fraud, searches for will beneficiaries. There was plenty of it and it kept his mind occupied, though he still brooded about the Todd case and how little impact he'd made on it, apart from adding another death that, but for his involvement, wouldn't have happened.

At lunchtime he saw Milly at the Fox and Grapes.

'How's it going, Frank?'

'Better than it was. How about you?'

'It helps to know I'll soon be finishing at The Fields. I've told Helen. She said the police have asked her to close for at least one night, so they can make a thorough examination of the debris of your motor. I've said I'll work a decent notice so she can find a replacement.'

'How did she take it?'

'Genuinely sorry to lose me, I think. Thanked me for my work and said she'd give me a good reference if I needed one. She was trying to take things in her stride like she always does. Poor Helen.'

'I need to see her later. Tell her I can't go on with a case that's too dangerous for a man working alone and which I'm pretty certain is insolvable, with the sort of people involved.'

'I'm glad, really glad.'

She was looking relaxed and well, despite the slight air of melancholy she carried round with her. Soon, she'd be able to abandon the tarty mask of make-up that seemed to paint her in colours that did nothing for the kind of woman he'd found her to be: kind, caring, intelligent and fun to be with. She always looked so right, with her normal delicate colouring in her turtlenecks and jeans. He felt she'd look good in office clothes as well, the long-line suit or the carefully chosen skirt and top. It would be a weight off her mind to be done with the casino and the sadness it had brought her, on top of the loss of her sister.

She put a hand on his. 'You'll stay ... over the weekend?'

'I think it'll be a good idea for both of us.'

She smiled. 'Just as a close friend, that's the agreement, isn't it?'

He nodded. He believed her. He sensed a realist. It would take her a while to get over the sort of man Todd must have been. When she *was* over him she'd want a man nearer her own age, and her instincts would tell her when the man came along she'd be able to spend her life with. There'd be no more Todds, he was certain. Or Cranes. And whoever she settled with would be one lucky man.

'Anyway,' she said, still smiling, 'I might want to call on your professional skills. I think I'm being followed.'

Crane, about to pour tonic into his gin, paused. '*Followed?*'

'I was driving along Lister Park's top road not long ago and my mobile rang. I checked the rear view and indicated to pull into the side. There was a man behind me with dark hair and heavy glasses, driving a Chrysler. It's a fairly unusual car and I remembered it being parked in Highgate one morning with the same man in it. And then, when I went shopping in town this morning I saw it when I turned off into the Co-op car park. He drove on. I suppose it could be just coincidence.'

But Crane was alarmed. Too much had happened around him and Milly. He didn't want her to pick up on his unease. 'Have you actually seen this man parked in Highgate since?'

She shook her head.

'That could mean he doesn't live in the area but has found out where you live,' he said calmly. 'If you see him one more time I want you to ring me. If you can memorize the number that would help. My friends in the force could supply me with an address. You'll do that for me, won't you?'

'I really don't think it means too much. It's happened before. One of the punters. I think he got a crush on me. I kept seeing him about at places I went to. He tried to make a pass, very politely. I blanked him. He followed me once or twice more but I kept on ignoring him. Then he disappeared.'

'Look, Milly, I know these things happen now and then to pretty girls. In fact I've been involved in sorting out one or two stalkers myself. But it can get unpleasant if they won't back off.'

'I'll ring you if it happens again.'

'Good girl. When was the first time you saw him?'

'About … ten days ago.'

This relieved Crane a little. Hopefully it was a simple stalking matter by a bedazzled gambler and had no connection to anything that had happened at The Fields. But he stayed uneasy. 'All right, Milly, if you see him again and can catch his registration number I'll sort it out. All it usually needs is a quiet word from a man my build.'

Later that afternoon Crane sat in his car keeping an eye on a house in Queensbury. The man who owned it was having his mortgage repayments covered by insurance, as he'd claimed he'd injured his back so badly in the heavy physical work he did that he could only get around on crutches or in an invalid buggy. The insurers suspected fraud. When the man, who was now steadying ladders against the side of the house, began to climb them with a paint pot and brush, Crane would be ready to take photos with a long-focus lens that would tend to prove the insurers had a point.

His mobile rang. 'Crane.'

'It's Pete Dexter, Frank. Can I see you?'

'Where are you, Pete?'

'At home. I have a place in Cottingley.'

'I could come over early evening, if you like.'

'The problem is, my partner will be back by then. I don't want to upset her more than she already is with Gerry being killed.'

'Do you know the Ramada hotel? Just the Bradford side

of the big new roundabout. Used to be called the Bankfield.'

'I know it.'

'I could see you there at six. We can sit in the bar.'

'I'll be there.'

Crane took several photos of the man on the ladder, now painting the landing window. 'Be careful, my friend,' he muttered. 'Don't want to make your back any worse.'

Dexter was waiting by his car in that section of the spacious tree-hung car park closest to the hotel. For the first time in Crane's dealings with him he looked very tense, even vulnerable. Crane took him through to the bar. He ordered a whisky and dry ginger for Dexter and a gin and tonic for himself and they sat at a small quiet table at the back of the room. 'Well, Pete…?'

'I've been with the police earlier this afternoon.'

'I was there this morning.'

'It was the man who was up there last night. Inspector Jones. He wanted to know about my dealings with Romano. I suppose you told him?'

'I have to put my hand up to that.'

'I told him about the job I'd been offered at Romano's casino. He said did I know Romano had a dubious reputation. I told him what I told you: if I took the job I'd just be there to run his casino.'

Crane wondered where this was leading. He said, 'Did Jones ask if you'd been in contact with Romano the night before last?'

Dexter's eyes shifted from his. 'I said I'd had no contact

with Romano since last Tuesday, when I was in his *salon privé* and you saw me there.'

'I don't think that was quite the exact truth, Pete, was it? You see, I thought it over very carefully and there were only two people I told I'd be at The Fields last night. One was Gerry and the other was you. I think we can rule Gerry out, apart from the fact that he's now dead.'

Dexter was silent for some time, sipping his whisky, eyes unfocused. In a low voice, he said, 'No, it wasn't the truth. Alphonse rang me the night before last. I might have mentioned you were seeing Helen last night. I had to tell him you'd seen me at his place. He never liked you being on the case. He wants Humph's killer found, or says he does, but I think what really bugs him was you maybe finding out about his little sidelines: the drugs, the laundering, all that.'

'Well *I* think what's really bugging him was me finding out that maybe he was involved in Humph's killing.'

'I swear I don't know one way or the other, Frank. It always looked like a drugs contract job to me.'

'I believe you. The problem with the drugs angle is that I found out early on there weren't any obvious reasons for there to be any bad blood between Humph and the Manchester people. But you should have admitted to Jones that you might have let it drop to Romano that I'd be at The Fields last night.'

Dexter fell silent again, picked up his glass and found it empty, gave Crane a contrite glance. 'I know,' he said at last. 'Since I left the station I've had the rest of the afternoon to think about it. That's why I felt I had to see you. When it

looked as if Alphonse was just doing a bit of snow and so on
I thought, well, Humph had scams of his own. What difference did it make who I worked for as long as they didn't
involve me in the dodgy stuff. But … well … killing people,
that's a different ball game. I don't know if Romano's
involved or not, but I've decided I'm staying with Helen. I'm
going up to her place when we've finished here to tell her
I'll accept her offer.'

'It's a good offer from a good woman, Pete.'

'I'm sorry I didn't come clean with Jones. Could you
square it for me? I think he's a friend of yours.'

'I'll speak to him. As you can see, your letting on to
Romano I'd be at the casino last night and my car being
blown apart last night is only circumstantial, but it could be
valuable evidence if a case was ever put together against
Romano.'

Dexter began to look intensely worried, if not scared. 'I
don't mind the police knowing the truth but if it ever came
to testifying in a court room, with types like Romano and
Billy Peddar around I don't think I'd even *make* it to a court
room.'

'The way things are I don't think anyone's ever going to
get around to feeling Romano's collar. He'll know every
dodge for making sure potential witnesses never get near a
box. But the police have to know about that phone call,
Pete. I'll square it for you with Jones, but he'll want to see
you again to get the facts exactly right. But he'll not be able
to take it any further without some absolutely clinching
evidence. Can I tell him you'll agree to see him again?'

Very troubled now and clearly having a struggle with his conscience, Dexter gave an almost imperceptible nod.

'Good man. Now this Billy Peddar bloke. He's the one who was with you and Romano in the *salon privé* last Tuesday?'

Dexter managed a weak smile. 'Romano's minder. Romano likes him around in staff interviews to get his reactions.'

'Know anything about him?'

'I decided right off it was best not to ask. But when we were talking generally Peddar said something like, "When I was in Derry...".'

'Northern Ireland. I'll bear that in mind. And now, if you're going up to Helen's place I'll go along too. I need to tell her I'm taking myself off the case. One reason is that I'm keen to stay alive and another is that I can't go on taking her money and coming up with nothing definite. It might have been Peddar and it might not but I doubt anyone's ever going to prove it one way or the other.'

Dexter looked slightly relieved.

Crane followed Dexter's Volvo up the winding roads to Helen Todd's fine house where it stood not far below the Bradford end of Ilkley Moor. They parked in front of the big garage, then walked past the window of the reception room where Helen had received Crane on his two earlier visits. The light of a mixed spring day had dropped now and the room was lit by table lamps. Helen, who must have heard the cars drive in, stood at the window looking out uneasily, arms folded. On their reaching the front door, she opened it herself. Crane said, 'Hello, Helen, could you spare us half an hour?'

'I very much hope you're not bringing me any more bad news, Frank. Hello, Pete. Do come in.'

She led them through to the spacious drawing room and waved them to sit. The men sat on one sofa, Helen on the opposite one. She was wearing her usual dark clothes, a black cashmere cardigan relieved by a string of pearls, a dark-grey skirt. She looked as pale and sad as ever, if not slightly lost looking. Crane guessed she must be wondering if her troubles would ever end. Well, at least most of the news they brought was good.

'Can I get you boys a drink?'

Crane glanced at Dexter. 'I think perhaps not, Helen, we've both had drinks earlier.'

'Yes, not a good idea with the limit so low now. I see some of our members drinking quite heavily, then climbing into their cars. I think, well, if they *want* to risk their licences that's their affair.'

'Perhaps it's the gambling instinct,' Crane said. '"Can I make it home without being breathalyzed?"'

It raised a fleeting smile on her wan features. 'Is there any news about that poor boy's death? His mother must be in a terrible state. He was her only child.'

'That's partly why we're here. But I'll let Pete give you his own news first.'

Her heavy eyes passed to Dexter's. He said, 'I've given your offer a lot of thought, Helen. I've decided I'd like to stay on at The Fields.'

Crane had expected to see intense relief but her expression remained oddly neutral. It might almost have been slightly indifferent. 'That *is* good news, Pete. I really don't know how I'd manage without you. We'll sort out the details when things get back to normal, if they ever do. If it's what Humph had in mind for the future I'm ready to go along with it. I only wish it were Humph sorting it out.'

Crane gave Dexter a sidelong glance. He too gave the impression he'd been expecting a more elated reaction. He said, 'I'm sure we'll be able to work out a deal we'll both be happy with.'

She sighed. 'I'm beginning to think I really will be ready to bow out before too long. This dreadful business with poor Gerry ... and knowing it was meant for *you*, Frank. I'm beginning to think that perhaps I need to get right away, try to make a new life.'

Crane felt it would be for the best. There were too many memories of Humph attached to the casino. She needed a long holiday, somewhere sunny, maybe a cruise. She was still an attractive woman and it could be there was some man out there who could give her the chance of a new happiness, even if Humph had been the sort of man she'd never really get over. 'I think that is a good idea, Helen.'

She said, 'I'm grateful to you, Frank, and I'm sure Pete is, for acting as go-between.'

'Too right,' Dexter said. 'Alphonse made me a good offer but I think I always really wanted to stay at The Fields. I've been with Helen and Humph all my working life.'

'Glad I could be of help,' Crane said. 'But this is the not

so good news. I don't think I can do any more work on Humph's death, Helen. It's just too dangerous for me now. If that poor chap hadn't been sitting in the car instead of me I'd not be here now.'

She watched him in a lengthy silence, nodded unhappily. 'It was too much to ask of you, Frank, I realize that now, with the sort of people who must be involved. I feel very bad about it. I let it become an obsession, felt I *had* to know who'd want to kill Humph. You're right, you mustn't expose yourself to any more risk.'

Crane said, 'If it brings anything for your comfort I think me, the police and Pete too are beginning to think very seriously that Alphonse Romano just might have something to do with the deaths.'

He told her about Dexter being one of the only two people to know Crane would be at The Fields the previous night and mentioning this to Romano. Her mouth had fallen open in shock, but there was fear too in her eyes, the fear that Romano's name always seemed to arouse in her when brought up unexpectedly. She began to shake her head. 'Oh, *Frank*, I really can't believe this can have anything to do with Alphonse, I really can't. He was our *friend*, mine and Humph's. He's been so kind to me since Humph … no, I really can't think …'

'He wants your casino, Helen. He's made his own casino an exact replica of The Fields. He knew I'd be at The Fields last night, knew I was looking into things and—'

'You must *stop* this,' she cut Crane off. 'I simply can't believe Alphonse … Yes, he'd love to own The Fields. But he's a businessman, ambitious. Yes, he's pushed me hard to sell to him, but that's what business people are *like*. I've done plenty of pushing of my own in the past. But he's always been a gentleman about it. Oh, *really* ...'

Her vehement defence of Romano took him aback. If Romano was such a kindly man why could he still see fear and tension in her eyes? 'Helen,' he said gently, 'all I'm suggesting is that there might be a possibility Alphonse has some *involvement* in the deaths. His knowing I'd be at The Fields last night and my car being blown up could be a total coincidence. Maybe the man who blew up my car kept an eye on The Fields *every* night, once he knew I was looking into Humph's death. I very much hope your friend isn't involved, but these details must be borne in mind.'

'Frank,' she said, on what seemed a note of near-desperation, 'you told me Humph was providing cocaine to some of the members. Well, if he was mixing with the sort of people who supply drugs, surely his death is more likely to be something to do with *them*?'

She was very agitated now. It made a startling contrast to her usual dejected composure.

'All along I've been inclined to think that way myself. And that might still be the case. I very much doubt if any of us will ever know.'

She sat in another silence, as if striving to cope with the carefully neutral comments he'd made about Romano, her and Humph's good friend of long standing. Finally she said, 'I need a drink. Are you sure you chaps won't have one?'

Crane got up. 'Let me get it. Brandy, is it?'

'Thank you. The kitchen's across the hall. There's a bottle on one of the worktops.'

He poured her a stiff measure in a large, airy room, full of state of the art equipment, together with an Aga and a vast American fridge-freezer. Crane's kitchen would have fitted into the room three times. On one of the walls was a portrait-type framed photograph of a man with thick, wavy, greying hair, strong features and lips parted on regular teeth in a warm smile. There were words written across a corner, 'To Nell, all my love.'

'You *were* a handsome beggar, weren't you,' Crane muttered. But even in the carefully posed photograph he was given a powerful sense of the man's vitality and felt a genuine pity that someone with such magnetism and drive should have had his life thrown away in such a squalid manner. He probably *had* loved Nell, despite his bits on the side. He'd known several men in his time who'd had bits on the side and whose marriages had been rock-solid.

He went back with the brandy. The pair were talking quietly. He put down the drink and said, 'I really think it would be best if you both put all this trouble out of your minds and made a new start. I'm an old CID man and this affair has got no-no written all over it.'

He thought he caught a flicker of comfort in her troubled face. He very much doubted she'd ever be able to bring herself to believe it could possibly have been that nice Alphonse Romano, dripping with his Italianate charm who could have had the remotest thing to do with the deaths. Perhaps she was relieved to know her incredulity was unlikely ever to be put to the test. She sipped her drink. 'Well, thanks, Frank, for all your hard work. I really am sorry I set you such an impossible task.'

'I'm only sorry it had to end with nothing achieved.'

'You've given it such a lot. I'll always feel guilty for exposing you to such appalling risk.'

'The risk came from the work itself, not from you.' He got up. 'Well, I think that's about it, so I'll be on my way.'

'Me too, Helen, if that's all right.'

She nodded almost ruefully, as if sorry to see them go. 'I'll see you when we reopen, Pete. I really think it best if we stay closed until Monday. The police should be well clear by then. I'm sure you've taken it on board that the takings are certain to drop for quite some time.'

'I have, but I *know* punters. I reckon inside a week we'll be back to normal. I daresay it'll take a while longer until the restaurant's fully on stream. Anyway, don't worry about it and have a good rest over the weekend.'

'I'll try, but what I'd give for a good night's sleep. Goodbye both. You must come up to the casino for a meal sometime, Frank, you and your partner, if there is one.'

'Thanks, I'd love to.' The men walked to their cars.

'Well, Pete, I'll wish you all success for the future. I doubt you'll see me again.'

'Thanks for your help, Frank.' They shook hands.

'Just one thing. Why does Helen seem to get nervy and tense when Romano's name crops up? It's happened several times when I've been with her. And if Romano's supposed to be an old buddy ...'

Dexter shrugged. 'I really couldn't say. He always comes over as a really likeable bloke. You can't help taking to him. But there *is* something else about him you can't put your finger on. There's no doubt he's set his mind on owning The Fields. It's maybe that when he wants something badly, even though he's ladling out the charm, he somehow gives you this sneaky feeling that it would be as well not to piss him about.'

'Terry Jones.'

'It's Frank, Terry. Does the name Billy Peddar ring any bells?'

'Should it?'

'He's Romano's minder. It seems he was once in Northern Ireland and I wondered if he might have had any links to the IRA or the Loyalists. I'm thinking in terms of car-demolishing skills.'

'I'll have a word with the super. He has contacts everywhere. You think this Peddar bloke saw to your car and Todd's?'

'Just an idea.'

'Leave it with me.'

'One more thing. Pete Dexter's been in touch with me. He's been thinking things over. He admitted to me he'd mentioned to Romano I'd be at The Fields on Thursday night.'

'Did he now? I suspected the sod was lying, though I have to say he's good with the poker face.'

'He's not a wrong 'un, Terry. He was just getting in too

171

deep with the Italian. Anyway he won't be working for him, he's staying on at The Fields. I think he's glad to be out of Romano's pocket. I told him I'd square it with you about him being economical with the truth. He's agreed to see you again. But I'm pretty sure he'd brick it if it ever came to testifying against anyone.'

The other sighed. 'You and me, we've been round the block. Can you see anyone *ever* going in a box for these murders? I reckon Dexter can sleep easy. But I'll have him in, for the record. Must go through the motions, eh?'

Crane hung up the wall phone. He was standing in the kitchen of Milly's house as she mixed the drinks.

'I thought you were supposed to be off the case,' she said, smiling. 'You do realize you're now working for nothing.'

'I owe Jones, Milly. Now and then he finds me good jobs I can do as a private man that the police have tended to put on the back burner. It's not that I'm any better but I can give a case more in-depth scrutiny if the client's ready to pay. I'm a fresh mind. I'm CID-trained and I don't need to stick to a rule book. And, to be honest, when a case like this comes along I tend to live and breathe it. I find it near impossible to let go.'

'Even when you nearly get blown up?'

He smiled. 'I'm not pretending that people who get as obsessed as me are entirely right in the head.'

She handed him his glass. He'd opened a bottle of Nuits St Georges which was airing on the worktop. Milly had a chicken casserole in the cooker that smelt delicious. He said, 'I've not smelt anything that smelt as good as that since I lived with Mum and Dad. It tends to be steak or pork chops or wall to wall M and S readies at my place.'

'I thought I'd do something a bit different, not having to go to the casino.'

She was a nice kid. Not only pretty and intelligent, but a good cook too. He was glad he'd agreed to stay over the weekend, even though he spent most Saturday evenings with Colette. Colette wouldn't know and wouldn't mind if she did know. The agreement from the start had been that they lived their own lives. Maybe one day they'd want a closer relationship but not yet. He'd needed Milly for this short time and she'd needed him. She'd been there for him when he'd been in the near-catatonic shock of being within minutes of being blown apart; he'd helped her, he felt, to finally come to terms with her double loss, to stop endlessly postponing the rebuilding of her life.

'Shall we take the drinks through?' she said. 'This needs to simmer for another half-hour. I'm so pleased you're staying over. I owe you.'

'Believe me, the debt's all mine.'

They sat together on one of the corner sofas in the living room. 'This bloke,' he said, 'the one in the Chrysler. Have you seen him since?'

'No. I've looked out for him, but nothing. I'm beginning to think it really was a coincidence.' She grinned. 'A real one this time, not like when you *pretended* it was a coincidence when our paths crossed in Highgate that first time.'

It still gave Crane a slight problem. He didn't believe genuine coincidences happened all that often.

*

Wendy, Dexter's partner, had gone into the house as he was putting the car in the garage. He turned off the lights, the radio and the engine and sat for a moment, thinking about his decision to stay on at The Fields. He was sure it was the right thing to do, and hopefully Helen would now be able to get Alphonse off her back. She'd made a firm decision to keep the casino with Pete as her partner and manager. Wendy was delighted they'd not have to move to Scarborough. They'd done so much to this semi: a new kitchen and bathroom, plans to extend the dining room out at the back. Yes, they'd made it into a really nice home. It would be a pity not to have the benefit of the alterations for a few years. But one day he wanted to think in terms of a place like Helen's up near the moors. Those big rooms, the views! He gave himself five years to be able to afford a mortgage on a house like Moor Rise. He got out of the car and flicked the doors locked with his key fob. It was nice having a break from the casino for a couple of nights, take Wendy out for meals.

He swung down the garage up-and-over, locked it. He'd have to tell Alphonse soon. He wasn't looking forward to it. Alphonse would conceal his disappointment in his usual pleasant way but he'd be taking it very badly. He'd ring him on Monday, put it out of his mind for the weekend.

He heard a step behind him, gave a wry grin. It would be Wendy, she would have left her handbag on the back seat once more. He'd have to unlock everything again. He turned. 'Oh … it's you. What are *you* doing here?'

'This is just a little warning, Dexter, to keep well away from the police. Well away. You know what I'm saying?'

Before Dexter could speak he got a fist in the belly. As he bent forward, groaning, he got a fist in the face. There were more blows and kicks and when he really came to he was in the A & E.

E L E V E N

'**P**ete! What *happened?*'

He had now been transferred from the A & E and found a bed in a ward. 'They reckon ... I'll be all right,' he said in a near-whisper. 'Cracked cheekbone, insides shaken up ... They say ... they'll clear up ... few days.'

There was bruising round his eyes and one side of his face was swollen. Speaking was obviously painful. Crane had passed a PC standing out in the corridor.

'Who did it, Pete?'

'I've ... told the police ... didn't see his face.' He winced on every word. 'I said ... just some nutter ...'

'But you do know who it was?'

'Billy ... Peddar. Said ... said to keep away ... from police. I'm ... I'm not ... naming him ... to Jones, Frank. And he can forget ...' The struggle was too much and he lapsed into painful silence.

Crane patted his arm. 'I'm sorry about this, Pete, I really am. There can only be one reason why Romano doesn't want you talking to the police.'

'Christ knows ... how they knew ... I'd *seen* the police. They must ... be following ... us around.'

A disturbing thought came into Crane's mind of a man in a Chrysler, who might or might not have been shadowing Milly. Maybe he was somehow shadowing them *all*, changing cars now and then and perhaps his appearance.

'You could be right, Pete. Well, if it's any consolation, I doubt Peddar will be back. I reckon he's given us both what he'll see as a gypsy's warning. They're going to believe we're not even going to think about who might have killed Humph and Gerry.'

'In my case ... they'll be ... absolutely ... fucking right,' Dexter croaked feelingly.

As Crane went back along the corridor a young woman was talking to the police constable. She held a plastic cup and her hair was untidy. She looked as if she'd not slept for twenty-four hours. He guessed it would be Dexter's partner; the look of hate she gave him seemed to prove it. Not only had Gerry been killed but now her boyfriend had been given a frightful kicking, all since Crane had come on the scene. It had happened to him before. He'd have to live with it, but it wasn't easy.

'Terry Jones.'

'It's me again, Terry.'

'About Dexter. I know. We can get nothing out of him. Never seen the guy before, di-dah, di-dah.'

'It was Billy Peddar. Dexter told me but he'll not tell you.'

Jones sighed. 'Tell me about it. "We're not keen on you

talking to the bogies and we're kicking your head in as a gentle reminder.'"

"'And if you go on being a naughty boy we might have to blow your wheels up, once we've made sure you're actually in them.'"

'Thank God you weren't in that car, Frank, though I'm really sorry about young Bishop.'

'And he died before he might, just might, have been able to give me a worthwhile lead. Well, it's water under the bridge now. Todd's death, Gerry's death, Dexter's kicking, it's all got to be down to Romano, and Romano will be fireproof. Romano comes from a race where the Mafia even have politicians in their pocket.'

'Where does it all end, Frank?' Jones said heavily. 'Drug barons, terrorists, suicide bombers, kids like wild animals on skunk and lager that's cheaper than water, stabbings, shootings. I tell you, if society can't protect itself against these people, by whatever means it takes, it's got too sophisticated and politically correct for its own bloody good.'

Crane gave a crooked grin. Once, after much soul-searching, he and a colleague in the CID had quietly tweaked some evidence against Bradford's criminal number one. The fix had been spotted by the villain's costly defence team. Crane had put his hand up and kept his colleague out of it as Ted Benson had children and a sick wife. That had been the end of his career in the force, though there'd been enormous sympathy for him and Terry Jones had given him a great deal of discreet help in the early days to help set him up as a PI.

'Well, if anything worthwhile comes up I'll give you a bell, Terry, but I doubt anything will now.'

'Yes, keep in touch, old son.' Jones put down the phone. He knew Crane, knew he'd fret about this case for weeks. That was how he'd always been in the force about any case he couldn't put a lid on. It was why he'd been the best man Jones had ever had on his team. He never stopped wishing he was back.

Milly had had a really nice day. She'd met Frank at the Fox for lunch and then she'd driven up past the golf links, parked in the car park opposite and then taken a walk through North Cliff woods and back over open fields. It had been a mixed day of fast-moving cloud, sunlight and an occasional spotting of rain, and she'd exulted in the clear, clean-washed freshness you got in an English spring, and in knowing she'd soon be out of the casino and hopefully starting a new chapter in her life.

It was now early evening and she thought they could have something for dinner that was fairly simple, like soup and maybe Spanish omelettes and crusty bread. She knew Frank wasn't remotely fussy about food and would eat anything she put before him with every appearance of enjoyment. He was working, of course, even though it was Sunday. It would have been nice to have had him walking with her as they'd walked along the cliffs at Scarborough. She'd begun to accept that he never stopped working. He didn't do holidays and he didn't do weekends.

She smiled, gazing through her kitchen window over her

lovely forsythias, she'd never seen them so full of blossom. She wondered where she'd read that sharks could never stop moving or they'd drown. They had to keep endlessly moving forward to force water through their gills. It was as if Frank, should he ever stop working, would drown in that sea of wry disillusion she sensed he lived in. She somehow knew that his work in the police force had meant such a lot to him, she wondered why he'd left. She also had an idea there was some woman he couldn't get over, who wasn't the one called Colette. She'd liked to have known what the story there was, too.

But he was a good sound bloke. He'd not been the one to make a pass that night in Scarborough, that had been her. And he'd been a considerate lover. He'd begun to temper her cynicism about there being any decent men left out there. He really had given her new hope.

She supposed she'd used him. She thought such a lot about him but knew it was no more than that. She knew the real longing was for a man more her own age, someone who didn't need to bury pain in endless work, someone she could party with, have holidays with, share a life and have kids with. Frank had been a sort of catalyst, someone who'd helped her to redefine herself. She would always be grateful for that.

But it hadn't been a one-way street and she was glad. He was a big strong man but she'd awoken on Thursday night to find him quivering in her arms and crying, 'Get me out! For Christ's sake, get me *out* of here!' No guess-work needed to know what the nightmare had been about.

She was glad she'd been able to give him comfort when he'd needed it most. They'd been a lifeline for each other and she was going to miss him when he went. And this would be her last night with him, but she felt she could now face the future with guarded optimism.

The phone rang. 'Milly, it's Frank.'

'Hi, Frank. I was thinking of making a start on dinner soon. Will you be long?'

'Milly, this is very important. Can you see me at the Norfolk Gardens? Room eighty-four.'

'What are you doing there? And what's wrong with your voice?'

'I'm starting to develop a sore throat. Can you come right away? I'll explain when you get here. It's very important.' The connection was broken.

Mystified, she hung up the phone. What could it *mean*? Why was he in a hotel room? Was it something to do with the case he said he'd given up on? She supposed it was. You just didn't see Frank as a man who gave up on things.

She locked up her house and went to her car, drove as quickly as possible down to the hotel, which was central in the city, opposite the town hall. Parking wasn't a problem as there was a multistorey adjoining the hotel. She parked on an almost deserted floor, hurried into the hotel, bypassed reception and made straight for the lift. It was only when she was walking along the corridor that she thought about the room number. He'd put down the phone before she could check it. Had it been eighty-four? Or was it perhaps eighty-two or eighty-six? She was sure it had begun with an eight and ended even. She decided she'd better confirm it otherwise she might find herself knocking on wrong doors and she had a feeling Frank wouldn't want her drawing attention to herself. She keyed his mobile.

'Frank Crane.'

'It's Milly. Just checking the number. Was it eighty-four?'

'You're talking in riddles, Milly.'

'I'm at the Norfolk, that's where you said. I'm just not sure about the number.'

'Milly, I'm in Skipton. What's all this about the Norfolk?'

'What's … what's going on, Frank?' she said, her voice suddenly shaky. 'Someone … someone pretending to be you wanted me to come to the Norfolk. He … he said it was very important.'

'Don't go in any room at *all*, Milly.' Crane was now very agitated. 'Just turn and go back home. I'll see you at your place.' He tried to speak calmly but couldn't keep the anxiety out of his voice. 'Go now, Milly, right now.'

At that moment the door of eighty-four opened. 'Ah, Milly …' A man darted out of the room, took her arm in a firm grip and pulled her inside.

'You,' she cried, '*You!*'

The line at Crane's end went dead.

TWELVE

Milly had never been given such a shock in her entire life. She felt as if her heart would stop. She stared at him open-mouthed and wide-eyed and shaking uncontrollably, with a kind of fear she'd never known. Had he had a *twin*? He *had* to have had a twin! A totally identical twin!

He gave her the steady look and the warm smile that always made you feel he was giving you his total attention. Just like his twin. It *had* to be his twin.

'It's all right, Milly,' he said softly. 'It really is me, large as life. Your very own Humph. Here, let me get you a drink. G and T OK?'

He went to the chiller cabinet and took out miniatures of whisky and gin-and-tonic. Still feverishly shaking, she gazed at the man who'd been shot to death and then had his car torched, now calmly pouring drinks as if behind his bar at The Fields.

He handed her the glass. She didn't take it. He smiled, shrugged, put it down on a bedside cupboard. She felt as if she couldn't have moved if she'd tried, as if intense shock had closed down the part of her brain that controlled movement.

'It wasn't me in the Mercedes, Milly.'

Crane had been working on a complex life-style check. He sprinted to his car, jumped in, and made for the Skipton high street. A red light on the dashboard and a peeping sound told him he'd forgotten to fasten his seat belt. It was a sign of his great agitation; he buckled up as he drove. 'You,' she'd said. '*You!*'

Who was 'you' and why had she sounded so shocked? Who could 'you' possibly *be*? A 'you' who must have been able to give a fair impression of Crane's voice. Who, to do with the business at The Fields, could know him well enough to do that? There was only really Dexter and he could barely talk at all. Or walk. He reached the roundabout at the top of the high street but there was a traffic bottleneck. It had been a good spring day and people were driving back from outings in the Dales and Bolton Abbey. The traffic on the street itself was inching along as there was another roundabout at the bottom that was feeding in cars from the Ilkley direction. Crane, beating his hands on the wheel in frustration, was beginning to have that sensation he knew only too well, as if concentrated acid was seeping into his stomach. It would take him three-quarters of an hour to reach Bradford city centre. At the very least.

She sat on the edge of one of the twin beds, hunched, almost curled up, like some small animal terrified at the sensing of a lurking predator. She gazed at him again, as if still unable to believe it really was Humphrey Todd, a Humphrey still very much alive.

'Chill out, Milly,' he said gently. 'I know I've thrown you a hell of a shock, but you have to be up very early to get someone like me out to that learner-driver place late at night to do a deal that sounded just a bit, just a little bit, too favourable. Here, drink your gin, it'll soothe your nerves.'

She finally accepted the glass, swallowed half the contents.

'That's the way!' he said, using the phrase the old Humph had so often used. 'God, it's good to be with you again, Milly. I don't know how I waited so long.'

She tried to speak but nothing came out. She sipped more of the little that was left in her glass.

'Let me get you another one,' he said. 'You obviously need it.'

'It was ...' Her voice returned at last, as a croak. 'It *was* you I saw in Scarborough. I thought ... I thought I was having delusions.'

'Definitely me. I'd been following you around. You caught me in Scarborough when you suddenly stopped and looked back.'

'The ... man in the Chrysler...?'

He grinned. 'After nearly being outed on the coast I took to the dark wig and the horn rims.'

There were no disguises now. There was the fine head of wavy greying hair, the strong regular features, the deep-set blue eyes that had always given an impression they could see into your mind and be able to tell how attracted to him you were. He wore a blue-and-white-striped cotton shirt and blue silk tie and the grey trousers of the sort of perfectly cut suit he'd always worn at The Fields. His lean body still gave the impression it vibrated with an almost inexhaustible vitality.

'I was a bit worried about that Crane guy,' he said, a faint wryness diluting the grin, 'but when I found he was a gumshoe I figured he'd oiled his way in with you because of something he was looking into at the casino. *Both* casinos, mine and Romano's. What was all that about?'

She watched him in pale-faced silence. He'd got a lot together in a short time, but he'd always been a fast worker. He'd got it right, really, Frank had only chatted her up originally for his work, however it had turned out in the end. 'He was … trying to find out who'd killed you,' she said, and though her voice was low and hesitant it was now a little steadier. 'When … when we all thought you *had* been killed.'

'Who set him on?'

'Helen.'

'Typical.' He gave a short derisive laugh.

Milly's sense that she was still in a dream state lingered, but she knew that if she put a hand out to touch him it wouldn't pass through an apparition. 'If … if it wasn't you in the car, who … who was it?'

'Don't bother your head about that, honey,' he said, pulling a chair to face her and grasping her cold hands in his warm dry ones. 'Let's just say I know who arranged to stop me breathing.'

*

Crane had cleared Skipton and driven the few miles to the dual carriageway bypass where he was able to give his car the hub-caps. But however fast he drove it was going to take him some time to reach the Norfolk and anything could have happened. Who *was* 'you'? It *had* to have been someone known to her, but who could she know well who could have handed her such a shock? It had to have been someone connected to the case and who'd known how to impersonate him. He remembered then that there'd been a call to his office when there'd been no one in. No message had been left on the answer-phone. He'd assumed someone had keyed a wrong number. The message on the answer-phone to advise he was unavailable was in his own voice. He wondered if the man who'd impersonated him had recorded Crane's message so that he could then practise speaking in Crane's voice. Could that have been the man in the Chrysler? But she'd not *known* the man in the Chrysler. And it could have been the Peddar guy. She'd never known him either.

He thought of pulling into a lay-by, ringing the Norfolk and telling them that a woman was in danger in a room that might be eighty-four, but abandoned the idea. The receptionist would think he was some kind of weirdo and Milly might not be in any real danger; it was after all a hotel and not a private house. And he would only waste precious minutes, almost certainly to no avail. He sped on, flashing cars who were indicating to overtake not to think about it till he was past. Later, he was very glad he'd not tried to contact the hotel. It could have led to endless complications. Even more than there already were.

Milly slowly withdrew her hands from Todd's. Even now she felt she could sense that sort of tingling in them she'd seemed to feel in the past, as if energy ran from him like an electric current.

'Who ... who did arrange for you to ... to be ...'

'Alphonse Romano.'

She watched him in silence. He sounded very decisive.

'Frank ... Frank Crane, he thought it was more likely to be the drugs people. He ... he found out you were supplying cocaine.'

'They were *meant* to think it was the drugs people. The police, Crane.'

She became silent again. He drank some of his Scotch. 'It's a long story. There were two men ambitious to dominate the upper-crust end of the Yorkshire gambling scene: Romano and me. I never made any secret of it, but Alphonse did. And underneath that incredible charm Romano can lay on, the bastard was picking my brains. I'd done a lot of research into government plans for additional casinos. I never really believed the big Manchester Las Vegas-style casino would come off, not under a Labour government, and I was proved right when they pulled the plug on it. But I felt the sixteen or so smaller ones had a chance and I wanted the licence for any new Yorkshire ones that might be given the go-ahead. And gradually I wanted to buy out any other decent casinos in any good county areas, that I could do up like The Fields. I'd got a few bob to one side and I knew I could get the leverage. All right, I wanted to be an empire builder, but I'd be giving good value for money to the sort of people I'd always aimed for. I was cultivating the right MPs, donating to party funds, all that stuff.'

He looked past her, eyes unfocused, a slight sadness darkening his face. 'My big mistake, Milly, was to tell Romano what I was up to. He was supposed to be a close friend, we'd have the meals together, the late-night drinks. He was always very respectful about my plans, or pretended to be. He owned a couple of discos, two or three T-shirt casinos, you know, the seaside ones. I thought he was satisfied with those. He always pretended to be. And he would encourage me to go for the posher end, ladle out the praise for my ideas.'

His eyes had focused on hers again, his face had hardened. 'I began to realize when it was too late the big mistake I'd made making such a close friend of him. He quietly bought the big place outside Scarborough that pulls in the nobs. Not a word to me. I only got it through the grapevine that he'd bought it through a front man and employed the same design team I'd used to make his place a replica of mine: the lights, the décor, the prettiest girls in town, a restaurant with a starred chef. He snapped up another casino near Harrogate through another stooge before I could get a bid in, began getting in bed with the MPs. Obviously Romano's a skilled businessman who knows how to play hardball, but the extensive detailed planning had been mine, Milly, all mine. And sooner or later

I knew he'd not rest till he could get his hands on The Fields. The bullet I didn't get in the brain proves it.'

She sipped a little of the second gin he'd given her. So *that* was how it had been. She wished she could think a little more clearly about what he was intending to do now, about how she could get herself away from here and back to some kind of normality. But the old attraction was still there, as if to cruelly taunt her. Maybe it had never really gone, even when passion had turned to bitter hatred because of that other appalling truth she'd learnt about him. She could remember so clearly those hands that seemed to tingle caressing her naked body. But very soon after that she'd heard ... She said, 'Why ... why did Romano think you'd *go* to the learner-driver place?'

'A good question.' Todd compulsively took her hands. again. 'He knew I discreetly ran a bit of coke. He'd got me the original contact. He comes from a long line of Italian crooks, he knows everyone there is to know in any kind of organized crime. I reckon he called in a favour from the man who sold me my stuff. He asks this guy to ring me and tell me he's just had a delivery of the best Charlie he's ever handled and do I want to be cut in on the deal. There's just the one problem. The bloke who'll bring the gear to Yorkshire has an idea the police keep tracking his wheels. He doesn't want to lead them to my place, so can we meet up at this isolated spot he's found on the outskirts and he'd be able to lose anyone who tried to tail him. It sounds more or less kosher till I start to think it over. That's when I decide it's got a bit of a funny smell. So I don't go.'

'Who … who was it in the car then?' she asked for the second time.

'Don't ask, darling. These are vicious people and whoever bought it in my place deserved it.' He gave her the adoring look she'd once not been able to get off her mind. 'Let's talk about *us*. Come away with me. We'll leave the country, start a new life together.'

Shock followed shock. How thrilled she'd once have been to have heard those words, even though she'd known he was a man who'd had affairs. 'There's never been anyone like you,' he'd told her back then. She'd really believed he meant it. Around that time she was aiming to invite him home, so they could spend most of the night together. And it had been around that time that Humph's car had been torched, apparently with Humph in it. And of course since then she'd learnt that other frightful truth about him.

She said, 'But you're supposed to be dead. Helen's been terribly upset. The police are bound to find out—'

'Milly, I just can't come back to life as the man I was. The minute Romano cottoned on he'd not rest till he'd had another go and he'd not leave anything to chance this time. There'd be endless complications about who really did die in my car. I've got plenty of money off-shore, not just part of the casino profits, but the coke money and a bit of discreet laundering. I've already given myself a new ID and a passport to go with it is being prepared as I speak. We could go as soon as you're ready. Somewhere nice and sunny. I could make a brand-new start with another casino. I know the business backwards and I've still got plenty of energy and optimism. And as for Helen, we've lived separate lives for years. We've only stayed together because we needed each other's skills. Otherwise it was an open marriage.'

'Humph, she's been in a terrible state since—'

'Only because she hadn't got me running things any more. She'll sell out to Romano, you watch. She'll be a wealthy woman.'

He squeezed her hands. 'So how about it, darling? Inside a couple of weeks we could be in the States, Australia, anywhere in Europe, you name it. Nice place with a pool, nice car, clothes, anything you want. You know you're the only girl for me. The first night you walked in the restaurant I *knew*. I never believed all that stuff about love at first sight, but boy, did Milly Brown prove me wrong.'

There were only a few miles to go but there were now sets of lights on Bradford Road to slow him down and leave him drumming his hands on the wheel again. There was so much *traffic*. Bloody day-trippers! He wasn't a man who tended to lose his cool, but this was Milly in a room with 'You'. Had she been forced in? Was someone trying to get from her what she and Crane had found out, not that they'd found out much anyway. Was 'You' going to knock her about, hotel room or not? He sped through a light that had just turned to red, heard the squeal of tyres, the blare of a horn. He cursed himself for an utter fool. There could have been a collision. He could have had points on his licence. He could have been badly injured. What was *happening* to the kid?

*

Milly found herself believing him, that he'd been as much in love with her as she with him. It wouldn't have lasted, she knew that now. He was just too attractive, knew only too well how attractive women found him to be. Once she'd have given anything to be magically whisked abroad with him, but she knew it wouldn't have been very long before the passion and the happiness had been replaced by the lies and evasions, the other women. The time since he'd 'died' had given her perspective. It had also given her a great deal of anguish that the 'death' had left her with so much bitter anger that could never find release.

She watched him in silence. She was slowly getting used to the fact that he really had cheated death, that this handsome man in these elegant clothes really was the man she'd once loved to distraction. And as the shock of surprise began to fade she could sense the return of that old quivering rage. How could she once have loved and loathed someone with an equal intensity inside a single day? Even now she felt she was having to cope with an illusion of the same dilemma.

He was still gazing at her with what in him she felt really did pass for love. 'Come on, Milly,' he said softly, 'what do you say? We could go into business together, like Helen and I did. You're bright, a hard worker. A big new venture.'

'I don't know, Humph,' she said slowly. 'There's still too much about all this I don't understand.'

'There's not much *to* understand. Romano lives in a

simple world. You want something you go out and get it, and if someone's in the way, too bad.'

'I know, but someone was killed in your place. I just feel I should know who it was.'

'Sweetheart, it was me or him.'

'You didn't really need to go to that place at all. Or send someone else there.'

'Milly, if what I felt might be a trap *was* a trap I had to be certain. So I played them at their own game.'

'I'm sorry, Humph, I have to know. We have to be honest with each other if ... if ...'

He gave her a puzzled look, unable to see why she felt she had to know the sordid details. She wasn't entirely sure herself why she had to know. Maybe it was the final uncertainty that lingered in her mind. Could this man she'd once adored really do these kinds of things? Coldly arrange for someone to die in his place? If he could it only confirmed in her heart and mind the type of man he was.

'You're best not knowing,' he said, in a low voice. 'It was a nasty business, but these were nasty men.'

'I *have* to know, Humph, so I ... so I can decide ...'

He sighed, ran a hand through his hair. 'It was one of their own people,' he said slowly. 'The drugs people. And that's *all* you need to know.'

'How could one of their people be in your car?'

'He thought he was doing me a favour,' he said, on a note of exasperation. He drained his glass. 'Oh, if you *must* know, it was a bloke called Liam Brent. He was the one who normally delivered the coke, but he was having a few days off and staying at Gerry's place. He was gay too. He'd come along in the evening, eat in the restaurant, play a little blackjack. I told him his people were sending this package of coke along, but I had to cover for one of the part-time inspectors. Could he take my car, which they'd be able to identify, and pick up the package for me. There was a satnav to guide him to the area and there'd be an earner in it for him.'

'But … but if the drugs man was from the Manchester gang he'd *know* Liam wasn't you.'

'Exactly. So he'd hand over the coke and that would be fine. But if it *wasn't* one of his Manchester friends, if by any chance it was one of Romano's people, or *anyone* who wanted me dead, well that man wouldn't *know* Liam wasn't me. He'd think whoever was in my car had to be me.'

She began to feel sick, started trembling again. She'd seen Liam Brent at the casino, had dealt him blackjack cards, had known he was Gerry's boyfriend. Gerry had always looked so happy having him around. And to be sent so callously to die. Todd cupped her face in his hands. 'He was no loss to anyone, Milly. The game he was in, the people he mixed with, his chance of losing his life was always evens anyway.'

She took his hands from her face. She wished to God he'd stop *touching* her, she couldn't bear it. 'He was a big loss to Gerry,' she said quietly.

'Gerry shouldn't have been fooling around with a drugs runner. Look, it's *done* now. This is where we're at. At the end of the day all you've got that really belongs to you is your body.' He now took her shoulders in his hands. 'Let's put it all behind us. Where in the world would you like to go? I ordered a room service meal for us before you arrived. A nice meal, a glass of wine ...'

She felt nauseated to the point of retching at the idea of food. She took his hands from her yet again, hands that had once seemed almost magical in the sensations they could arouse in her. She got up, began to move distractedly about the room.

'It must have become easier,' she said harshly, 'letting a drugs runner die when you'd left Sophie to die in a Jacuzzi.'

THIRTEEN

They were wiped away, the tender smiles. Shock had made his face as pale as if he'd had heart surgery. He couldn't get a word out for several long seconds. 'Sophie ...' He finally spoke in a voice suddenly hoarse. 'Sophie *who?*'

'My sister, Sophie Brown.' Her mouth was so dry that she too found it difficult to speak. 'I don't suppose you knew her surname, did you, seeing as it would be Helen who'd have set her on in the restaurant?'

'What ... what's that got to do with *me?*' He stared at her, wild-eyed. 'This ... this Jacuzzi business?'

'You began taking her out, yes, just like you did me. She was a fun-loving girl, my sister, and she could seem a bit too friendly, and the wrong men sometimes got the wrong impression.'

He was still looking dazed, still stared, but she sensed his knife-edge instincts for handling upsets around women were warning him to think carefully before speaking again. Finally he said, 'You gave me such a shock. I could never have guessed you were her sister. I'm so sorry, Milly. Of course I remember Sophie … and her frightful death. The police came but all we could tell them was that she'd gone home at the usual time. I'm so very sorry.' He got up, tried to hold her again, but she brushed him abruptly away. 'But … but why do you think *I* was involved? I barely *knew* her.' His pallor was being replaced by a slight flush. 'She'd only been with us a few weeks.'

She said, 'When I was beginning to get over the dreadful shock of her death I decided to try and get a job at The Fields. You made it easy for me as it turned out.' She couldn't bring herself to look at him as he was putting on the tender smile again that came so easily to him. 'I wanted to know if anyone knew anything, anything at all, about how Sophie could have ended up at the house in Hawksworth that night. I could never have believed it was anything to do with you. Not ever. Well, you know how I was about you.' She couldn't control a half-sob.

'*Milly*,' he said warmly, self-confidence returning by the second, 'how could you possibly imagine I had anything to do with poor Sophie? I've had affairs, I never pretended otherwise, but I barely knew Sophie. How can you possibly think I was involved?'

'Because Gerry Bishop overheard you!' she cried. 'He had back trouble. It eased the pain if he could lie down now and then. He was lying down in the dark behind the desk in the interview room when you came in. You didn't put the light on and you rang a man called Morgan on your mobile. You asked to borrow his place again. You and a few friends wanted to have a bit of fun with a scrubber.'

Todd's returning colour ebbed again. She said, 'Gerry should have told the police but he couldn't bring himself to, not right away. By the time he could you were dead, or supposed to be.'

She was suddenly overwhelmed by a wave of such distilled anger that she was able to meet his eyes now in a stare of cold fury. It was his gaze that dropped now, his hands that began to shake. 'He loved you too, you see,' she flung at him. 'He loved you like a father. He couldn't believe you'd left my sister to drown in a Jacuzzi after you'd all raped her. He could only bring himself to tell me when he believed you were dead.'

'Milly ... Milly ...' His voice held a pleading note. 'You can't think I'd involve myself in that kind of a scene....'

'You were *there*! At Morgan Walker's house with some of your high-rolling friends. Men you could trust, men you did favours for. Walker was conveniently away from home. Sophie had thought it was just going to be you and her somewhere where you would be alone. When she found there were other men there and no women she would have got very angry – and she could get very, *very* angry if she thought men were trying to treat her like a tart.'

'She *was* a tart!' he suddenly shouted. 'Think I'd have taken her to a session like that if—'

'She was *not* a tart!' she screamed. 'She liked men and she liked fun and I had to keep an eye on her because men often got the wrong idea, but she knew how to deal with men who thought she was a pushover. But she couldn't deal with a bunch of men when her drink had been spiked.'

'She took the drugs herself! That's why it all went wrong, because she'd OD'd.'

'Sophie didn't do *drugs*! I knew everything about her, we'd not been out of each other's sight since we were babies. She got furiously angry that night, yes? And when you began to realize she wasn't the pole-dancing ratbag you'd taken her for you apologized and gave her a drink to calm her down. Only the drink was spiked. And then you all raped her and when you were beginning to come down from your own highs you saw she was injured and bleeding. You panicked then – yes, you could see prison sentences all round, and when she dragged herself to the Jacuzzi and fell in you just left her there and pissed off home. I'm sure you can put me straight on any little detail I've not got quite right.'

She burst into tears then and wept, as she'd so often wept in the past at the loss of her other self. Todd sat down again on the edge of a bed and put a hand to his forehead. Through her blurred vision he seemed to have aged in the past minutes; appeared gaunt, hollow-eyed.

'Milly,' he said at last in a low voice, 'all right, I took her to Hawksworth. I …well, I thought she was up for it. We'd all have made it worth her while. But … you have it right … she got very angry. She was given a drink to calm her. I'd no idea it had been spiked, I *swear* it. I tried to stop the others from … doing what they did, but … well, they'd all had a line or two. I told them I was out of it. I never did anything to Sophie. That's the honest truth. I went outside, tried to decide what to do. When the others began clearing off I went back inside. I was going to stay with her till she was over the drug. I was going to beg her to forgive me. If she'd not report it I'd give her as much money as she needed to be able to do whatever she wanted to do with her life.

'But … but she was lying in the Jacuzzi. I … I knew she was dead. I can't begin to tell you how sorry I am.'

She watched him. His voice held the convincing note that was an exact match of the one that had been there when he'd admitted to having had affairs in the past, but had insisted again and again that she was the only woman he'd ever loved.

'Well, Humph,' she said, in a voice that was low but steadier now, 'I shall leave it to the police. They'll have the DNA samples they took from my sister's body. They'll be able to sort out exactly who did what.'

'Milly … darling Milly, let's move on now. I've been a fool and I'm ashamed of myself, but you must believe I personally didn't touch Sophie—'

'But you bottled out of telling the police.'

'I said I'd been a fool. And the police think I'm dead anyway. If you can begin to try and forgive me I'll take you away from all this and we can live—'

'The police won't think you're dead once I've assured them you're still alive. And then you'll have *two* murders to talk over with them, won't you? And you'll not be able to settle this with a fistful of money.'

'You can't do this to me, Milly. You know how very much I love you, don't you? We'll go away. A nice sunny climate. In a month this will all seem like a bad dream.'

201

'You'll very soon know more than you ever really wanted to know about bad dreams,' she said evenly. 'The police will have the truth as soon as I'm out of this place.'

She knew, in part of a second, that those last words had been a dreadful mistake. His face slowly began to harden and he watched her with the coldest eyes she felt she'd ever seen. She sensed she was seeing something in his face of the man he really could be, the man he'd always previously concealed from her. 'Well,' he said softly, 'I'll just have to make sure you don't get out of the place, won't I?'

Andy stood outside eighty-four with his trolley of food and wine: the warm plates under their cloches, the chilled champagne, the Bordeaux, the vacuum jug of coffee. It was always a pleasure to serve Mr Bradley, he was a really nice bloke who tipped generously. He tapped on the door. 'Room service, sir.' The door was flung open by a young woman. 'Quick!' she cried, 'keep him away from me! He's going to *kill* me! Keep him *away* from me!'

She plunged out into the corridor and along towards the lift. Todd dived after her but was stopped by Andy. Andy was big and strong and he held Todd in a firm grip. Todd said, 'Let me go, Andy. She's just overwrought and hysterical. I'll calm her down.'

Andy watched him carefully. He hated having to manhandle a guest, but the woman was half the man's age and very distressed. She could have been a call-girl. He'd once seen a call-girl come out of one of these rooms in a very battered condition and it was something the hotel could do without.

'You need to calm down too, sir,' he said. 'I'm sorry I've had to restrain you but the lady did seem very upset.'

Todd's lengthy experience of handling difficult situations warned him that struggling wasn't a good idea. Every second counted but he forced himself to give the waiter his friendly, practised smile. 'Sorry, Andy, but it's not what it seems. She's got herself into a state. We're an item. We'll be getting married just as soon as I can get a divorce. The kid thinks I'm not sorting it out quickly enough and she's threatening to go and see my wife and force the issue. That would not be a good idea, not with a wife like mine.' He gave the waiter a conspiratorial wink.

Andy believed him. Mr Bradley was too nice a bloke to knock a woman about. He took his hands from Todd. 'Sorry, sir, it was just with the lady saying you'd hurt her.'

'I had to stop her rushing off, Andy. If she got through to my wife the complications would be endless. She got me very cross and I said some silly things, I admit. I'll go after her now and talk her down. With any luck I'll catch her in the multistorey. Just take the trolley in and leave it. We'll be back.' A twenty-pound note had appeared in his hand, which he tucked into a pocket of Andy's waistcoat.

'Well, thank you, sir, and good luck.' He grinned. 'So glad you'll not be killing her, after all.'

'Andy, I couldn't harm a hair on that girl's head, not in a million years,' he said with a wide smile, then he set off rapidly along the corridor.

*

Minutes earlier, Crane had finally driven along Hall Ings and into the multistorey that adjoined the hotel. There were plenty of spaces, it being Sunday, and he parked quickly. As he doused the lights, turned off the engine and tore at his seat belt the silence seemed almost oppressive. And then a woman broke the silence, running across to her car. It was *Milly*! 'Thank Christ,' he muttered in relief, throwing open his door. But before he could get out she was already gunning the engine, and then there was a squealing of tyres as she fumbled the pedals. At that moment the door from the stair-well burst open and a man in shirtsleeves ran out on to the floor and towards Milly's car as it shot out on to the exit route. 'Milly!' he cried, 'don't go! You know I didn't mean—'

He ran towards the car, waving his arms for her to stop, but the Citroën, travelling at its optimum speed in second gear, surged on, hurling him aside. He was pitched head first against one of the load-bearing concrete pillars, then he slumped into the shadows between two parked cars. Milly drove on without a backward glance, out of the building, pausing only to activate the mechanism that raised the exit barrier.

Crane walked over to where the man had fallen. The silence was again intense. The man lay crumpled, his head at an ominous angle to his body, eyes staring sightlessly upwards. Crane felt in his neck, but knew he was dead. He'd attended too many car accidents when he'd been a uniform in the police force. There wasn't the flicker of a pulse.

He glanced round him. The floor was deserted. He went back to his own car, restarted the engine and drove out of the building. Had the man been alive he couldn't have abandoned him. But he was very dead, had been killed by Milly's car, and he needed to see Milly before he did anything else. Because the face he'd just seen, lit clearly by Crane's pen-type torch, had been the same face he'd seen on the framed photograph in Helen Todd's kitchen.

F O U R T E E N

She opened the door very slowly, on the chain, face pale and fearful.

'It's me, Milly.'

'Frank! Oh, thank God!'

She slid off the chain and let him in. He put his arms round her and she clung to him, her entire body shaking. 'He'd have killed me,' she whispered. 'He'd have *killed* me!'

He led her back into the living room, sat her on the sofa. 'I got to the multistorey just before you drove off,' he told her. 'You never saw me.'

'You saw him trying to stop me?'

'He's dead, Milly. His head hit a pillar. I checked him out. He's definitely dead.'

She sank back into the sofa. She looked weak with relief. 'It was ...' She broke off. 'Well, you're just not going to believe this, but it is the truth. It was Humphrey *Todd*!'

'I know. I'd seen a photo of him at Helen's place.'

She couldn't stop shaking. He went to the kitchen and mixed two gin and tonics. He put a glass into her trembling hands. 'Do you want to tell me how come he was still alive?' he said gently.

She began haltingly to tell him all she'd found out in room eighty-four. She backtracked, got things out of sequence and repeated herself, but in the end, with the occasional question, Crane was able to thread the barely credible story together. It took her a long time and when she'd finished she began to cry, for what he could tell was not the first time this evening. She was crying, he knew, for the sister who'd been like a twin and maybe for the man Todd had once seemed to be, combining warmth and charm with perhaps a hint of the fatherly qualities her own father had so rarely been able to provide.

She finally began to dab her eyes with a tissue, sipped some of her gin. Crane took her hands in his. 'When did Gerry tell you what he'd overheard?'

'Not … not long ago,' she said, in a voice now a little more under control. 'He was the only person who knew I was Sophie's sister. He'd had bad attacks of conscience when Humph was still alive. But he finally brought himself to tell me about Humph's involvement.'

'I suppose that's what he was going to tell me. Just in case Sophie's death and Humph's apparent death were connected. He should have told the police, Milly. And really, so should you.'

'Humph was supposed to be dead, Frank. There seemed no point in telling the police. All the details had died with him.'

'Well, you can't be blamed for not thinking like a

policeman,' he said gently. 'But the police would have got on to Morgan Walker again and put the pressure on. He'd know the types who were with Humph.'

'I didn't think it through, did I,' she said sadly.

'I'm not surprised, you had a lot on your mind.'

'And … and I'm sorry, but I couldn't bring myself to tell *you* what Humph had done. I just didn't want you to think I'd involved myself with a man who could do such a dreadful thing.'

'There are few minds broader than mine.'

'Oh, Frank, what do we do *now*? It's such an appalling *mess*. I didn't mean to *kill* him! I just wanted to get away.'

'I know, I know. And he'd have tried to kill you if you'd *not* got away. He knew if you'd lived he'd be facing the slammer. He'd also know the danger he'd be in from Romano.'

'I'll have to tell the police, won't I?'

Crane thought about this for some time. 'When you went to his room did you go through reception?'

She shook her head. 'It all seemed so odd I didn't think you'd want that. How could he imitate your voice on the phone?'

He told her about his idea that Todd had recorded Crane's voice from the answer-phone. 'So you went directly to his room and the only hotel employee who saw you was the man with the room-service trolley?'

'He only got a quick glance. Where … where's this going, Frank?'

Crane fell silent again for a little while. 'The way I see it, Todd had had several months to give himself a near-indestructible new identity. All connection with the man he'd been, totally obliterated. It'll leave the police nowhere: no wife, no partner, no friends, no enemies. But it's happened before. They'll find he had access to big money in off-shore accounts and they'll assume he was an underworld figure, anxious for any of a number of reasons to cut all ties with the man he really was. But, being run down in a multi-storey they'll assume his past caught up with him. A gangland job. My guess is they'll bung the details on file and quietly let it lie until something turns up by chance, if ever.' He patted her hands. 'The only person who saw what really happened is me and I'll not be speaking about it to any police.'

Her green eyes rested sombrely on his. 'I didn't *mean* to kill him but I can't pretend I'm sorry he's dead, not for what he did to Sophie and poor Gerry's boyfriend.'

'Put it out of your mind now, Milly. We should go to the police with the full story. I'm an ex-cop and maybe I thought the day would never come when I'd not do that in any circumstances. But not in these. The swine got the fate he deserved. Let's regard it as natural justice.' He gave a grim smile. 'And anyway, you can't kill a man who's already dead, can you?'

He drove once more on to the drive of Helen Todd's big house. The housekeeper answered the door and left him in the hall while she checked that Mrs Todd would be prepared to see him. She was and he was taken into the usual spacious reception room with its perfectly plumped cushions and polished furniture. Helen looked up from a sofa with the sad pale expression she did so well. It had certainly fooled him, along with everyone else.

'Hello, Frank,' she said in a low voice. 'What brings you here? I thought we'd had to accept that the case was finished.'

'I think it might just be starting, Helen,' he said evenly, 'for you.'

It handed her the shock he'd been aiming for. She couldn't stop her eyes widening in a look of what seemed to be a mixture of fear and anxiety. 'What are you *saying*?' she said uneasily. 'Does this mean you actually *know* who ... who did kill Humph?'

'Well, you knew from day one, Helen, yes? It was your boyfriend Alphonse, or at least his executioner, Billy Peddar.'

Her mouth fell open and the whites flared round the pupils of her eyes. She couldn't speak for long seconds. 'What can you mean,' she almost whispered. 'What can you possibly *mean*?'

'On the night I was almost killed, Helen, I asked myself who could have *known* I'd be at The Fields that night. Well, it was just the boys, Gerry and Pete. And it was Pete who told Romano, but for quite innocent reasons, certainly not to get anyone killed. But Romano used the information to *try* to get me killed.

'Let's move on to Friday, when me and Pete came to see you. Pete told you he was going to admit to the police he'd told Romano about my movements and that he suspected

Romano of killing both Humph and Gerry; Gerry of course being the poor sod who lost his life in my place. The following night Pete takes such a beating from Peddar that he's still eating hospital food.' Crane paused for a few seconds. 'And the only person who could talk to Romano this time, Helen, about Pete talking to the police was you.'

She was striving very hard to conceal the fact that she was having a lot of trouble with her breathing. 'What nonsense is this!' she cried. 'You've always had this obsession about Alphonse. I've never denied that he wanted The Fields. But he was *always* a gentleman about it. As for this ... this Peddar person, I've never heard of him.'

'I daresay Pete wishes he could say the same.'

'It was *dark* when Pete was attacked. He could have been mistaken!'

'How do you know it was dark?'

'I rang Pete at the hospital to offer my sympathy, ask if there was anything I could do.'

'How did you know he was *in* hospital?'

'His ... partner rang me. He'd be off work for a few days.'

She was lying and Crane knew that she knew that he knew. 'Helen,' he said, 'it was definitely Peddar and Pete's duffing-up was a warning not to speak to the police – about anything.'

She sighed and was silent for more seconds. When she began to speak it was in a calm and collected tone that he could only admire. 'Frank,' she said, 'Alphonse ... Mr Romano ... he owns casinos, nightclubs. I'll be honest, when all that money moves around the little scams do go on. It's part of the territory. So Alphonse does a little coke for the wealthy, maybe launders a little money through the *salon privé*. It's almost expected of him by some of the high-rollers. But none of us wants the Gaming Board or the Revenue breathing down our necks. I really think Alphonse was just worried Pete might let slip some details of his little arrangements to the police. I think he sent this … this Peddar person to have a discreet word with Pete and Pete took it the wrong way. Pete can be aggressive too, you know. You have to be able to watch your back in this business.'

'Nice try, Helen,' he said flatly.

'Oh, really, Frank!' He was still able to detect both anger and fear behind the composed mask she'd adopted. 'You've been round the block, you must know these things go on in the leisure industry.'

'Coke and laundering I can just about live with, it's people being assaulted and murdered I draw the line at.'

'But you really can't think Alphonse—'

'I don't just think it, I'm certain of it.'

'I simply can't begin to understand how both you and Pete can imagine that Alphonse had anything to do with those murders.' Her calm act of self-possession still held but he could sense it came at a heavy price.

He said, 'Let me give you my fix on it, Helen, now I've had time to think it all through. You fell for Romano, didn't you?'

'No,' she said, in an even tone, 'I just like him very much as a friend.'

'He came to The Fields a lot because he was bowled over

by what you and Humph had made of the place. He longed to own it, couldn't wait to get his hands on it.'

'I never made a secret of how much he wanted to own it.'

'But it became his obsession. He knew he'd get nowhere with Humph so he turned to you. Flowers, phone calls, meals at nice restaurants.'

'All right, I go out with him for a meal now and then. He's a *friend*.'

'But you fell for him. You told him a little coke-pushing went on at The Fields too, not knowing it was Romano who gave Humph the contact.'

She hadn't known that. The calm act couldn't entirely conceal her surprise. 'You see, Helen, that's how Romano could imply that Humph's murder was down to the Manchester drugs barons.'

'But it *was* the drugs people. A dispute over a poor quality consignment.'

'And it was Romano who put the idea in your head?'

'You yourself thought it was the drugs people at one stage—'

'And it was the drugs people who came back to blow up my car, was it? Drugs people don't *do* unnecessary murders, especially of a PI they couldn't even know about, as I did the Manchester enquiries through an agent. It was Romano who was getting edgy, about a detective who seemed to be getting a little further than the police.'

'You're so wrong, Frank,' she said coolly. 'If you could only *know* Alphonse, know him for the decent type he is.'

'It might have been best if you'd never heard him in

action. Like the chap in the *Odyssey* having his ears stopped against the sirens.'

She remembered enough of her schoolgirl Greek mythology to understand the allusion. She blushed slightly.

'Look, Frank—'

'How did Romano come to get the green light, Helen? What did you let slip? That you wished you could wave a magic wand and Humph would be out of your life? Wished him dead for all the times he'd cheated on you?'

'I didn't *mean* it!' she suddenly cried. 'You say silly things when you're unhappy.'

'Not to Romano you don't. Not at all a good idea.'

He'd somehow hit on the right choice of words. Her calm, collected act had gone, to be replaced by trembling rage. 'Humph this, Humph that!' she cried. '*Everyone* thought the swine was Mr sodding Wonderful. Well, he was till you got to know him. Yes, maybe I did once say to Alphonse I wished the swine was dead, but that doesn't mean Alphonse *killed* him.'

'It all begins to point that way.'

'Alphonse was just very *sorry* for me, that's all. I shall sell him The Fields and then become his partner. In every way. But that's because we love each other. It has nothing to do with Humph's death.'

'Humph's death was very convenient, you must agree.'

'I'm glad he's gone. Just glad he's gone. One woman after another and me slogging away helping to build up the casino, and then the restaurant. That restaurant was all down to me and what thanks did I get for it. The increase in *turnover*! I put off having children till it was too late just so's I'd not be distracted from the casino. He thought he was being so clever with all his women, thought I didn't know what was going on. Well, I knew *everything*, including that business up at—' She abruptly broke off.

'Up at Morgan Walker's place at Hawksworth?'

Another shock. The flushed features of the past minutes faded into pallor. 'How could you possibly know that? How could you?'

'I'm a CID-trained PI. I spent a lot of time looking into Humph's background.'

He had to go carefully here. Had she not been in such an emotional state she'd have wondered how he could possibly have linked Todd to the Hawksworth death.

'He deserved to die,' she said, in a low, raw tone. 'They saw to that poor bitch, didn't they, him and his fine friends? I can't prove anything, never could, but I just knew it was him. But Alphonse didn't kill him. Alphonse couldn't do a thing like that.'

'You've been fooled once by a charmer. Don't repeat the mistake.'

But his instincts told him she was the sort of woman who couldn't resist men like Romano and Todd. She was like those other successful women who played the tables, women who ran businesses and non-execed on other boards. They were all clever and tough, tough with that sort of shell that seemed to meet in the middle, but so often deep down there was a soft centre lurking there. They couldn't make do with weak or unsuccessful men and were dazzled by the achievers. And if the achievers had that overwhelming, carefully nurtured charm, any faults seemed to be lost in the glow. He was positive that in the early hours of what Scott Fitzgerald had called the real dark night of the soul, Helen Todd must have heard warning bells, however distant: two linked deaths and a man desperate to get his hands on her casino. And when he owned the casino would he still want her? When he had his choice of hand-picked call-girls?

'Look, Frank,' she said at last, back to the measured and reasonable tone she could slip on like a pair of well-worn gloves, 'don't forget, it was me who actually set you on to look *into* Humph's death. I may have begun to hate him but I felt I owed it to him to at least try to find out who might have been responsible. Why should I engage you if I believed Alphonse to be behind it all?'

'The police couldn't pin it on anyone. But you were extremely anxious for them to prove it *wasn't* Romano. So you hired me, a fresh mind, to see if *I* could prove it wasn't Romano.'

'I was shattered about Humph's death,' she said, as if she'd not heard his last words. 'You could see how upset I was. I'd stopped loving him but I'd loved him once. We'd had a lot of happiness building up the casino in the early days. I felt someone *had* to pay for his death.'

'Your mourning widow was flawless,' he said. 'It certainly fooled me for a very long time. I really believed in your pain, right up until twenty-four hours ago. That was when I suddenly remembered what I'd been told by your part-time inspectors, Bert and Max. They told me about your actress training, about being so good the *Emmerdale* people wanted to write your bit part into a central character. You deserve an Oscar for the class act you've put on since Humph died. You kept the rest under wraps; yes, the bitterness you must have lived with for years for having let go what might have been a brilliant stage career to marry Humph and work the clock round helping him fulfil *his* dream.'

He was so accustomed to her grieving widow act, the skilful way she could even hint at grief when she was being chatty and cheerful with guests in her restaurant, that it handed him a considerable shock to be seeing something of the woman she really was. She watched him in silence but her hands shook and her eyes were filled with what seemed a distilled bitterness. 'He was certain he could get me into films,' she said, in a low grating voice. 'Shaftesbury Avenue. My agent. He wept when I said I was going to marry that piece of shite and work in his betting shop. He *wept*! He said he'd never handled anyone with my potential, I was a natural. And what am I left with now when I could have been with acting people and living the life I really always wanted. A fucking *casino*.'

Silence fell and she began to cry. Not noisily, but letting the tears slide down her cheeks. Crane knew them for what they were, real, non-acting tears. She gazed towards him with unfocused eyes. He got up and went to the kitchen, where he poured her a stiff brandy. Todd's image looked down on him from the framed photograph, his smile seeming now almost like a sneer.

217

'Well,' Crane muttered, 'you've won, you bastard. You may be dead but when you were alive you never had to go through it like you made others go through it. You're out of it and scot free.'

But that was the tricky sod life was. He went back with the brandy. She quietly wept on. He handed her the glass, drew up a small table. She gulped a mouthful, put down the glass, then leant over to his chair and took both his hands in hers. 'What shall I do, Frank?' she asked him, in a voice that held a definite note of contrition.

'Well—'

'I so much wanted Alphonse to be what he seemed. I'd become so dreadfully unhappy with Humph.'

'Look, Helen—'

'He convinced me that Humph had had a dispute with the drugs people about poor-quality coke. He said he'd picked up that they were very upset about Humph owing them a lot of money.'

'And I suppose he told you that my intended death was because the drugs people thought I was getting on to *them*.'

She watched him, the sadness in her eyes genuine after the long weeks of sustained and brilliant acting. She nodded.

Crane said, 'A totally reliable source assured me that Humph was in no trouble in Manchester.'

'You were right,' she said, with a heavy sigh.' I was hoping you or the police *could* prove it was the drugs people. You can't begin to know how much I wanted Alphonse to be what he seemed. Just ambitious, good fun.'

She sipped a little more of the brandy. 'What do I *do*, Frank?' she said again.

'He's a dangerous man, Helen, but he knows every dodge for protecting himself. Everything we have against him is circumstantial, apart from Pete being beaten up by Peddar, and Pete isn't going to tell the police. The police just haven't enough to mount a case that would carry any weight with the CPS.'

'What … what should I do about the casino? If Alphonse continues…?'

'Keep it. You've put so much of your life into making it the place it is. With Pete as manager you'll have a lot of freedom.' He smiled. 'You could even have a crack at going back into acting. I'm sure there are still openings in *Coronation Street* or *Emmerdale* for an actress with a talent like yours.'

They sat over a drink at the Toll Gate. Crane had told Terry Jones everything that had passed between him and Helen Todd. Jones sighed. 'You're right, Frank, none of it stands up. Not even the extra stuff we've got on Peddar makes it any other than circumstantial.'

'What extra stuff would that be?'

'Had I not told you? This bloke the super knows in Belfast. He remembers Peddar very well, they always knew it was him when there was a Loyalist's car that needed demolishing. Peddar was an expert with explosives but he worked to a unique pattern, that's why the experts always knew it was his handiwork. He never used fertilizer and diesel as most tended to, always went for the sticks of dynamite. Well, they finally nailed the bugger in the early nineties, but when Tony Blair came to power the so-called political prisoners were released as part of the peace deal. This contact of the super's often wondered what became of Peddar. Well, they sent us a copy of the forensic details of Peddar's explosives technique and, surprise, surprise, they exactly match the details of the way your Renault was totalled. It gets us nowhere, even so.'

Crane began to feel the old familiar *frisson*. 'But it's looking good, Terry. When Todd's Merc was torched it had to have been Peddar, yes? He didn't need to bother with explosives then, just a straightforward, on-the-spot execution.'

'How does that help?'

'Because your men found a half-smoked cigarette butt in the long grass near the wreckage. The forensics got a DNA sample but couldn't match it to the database. Well, maybe Peddar went in the slammer before DNA was perfected. But you could bring him in now on suspicion and check if his DNA now matches the cigarette-butt sample.'

Jones shook his head in resignation. 'Christ, that memory of yours. I should have remembered that.'

'You supervise a hell of a lot of cases, Terry. I've lived just with the Todd affair for a fortnight.'

'If the DNA *is* Peddar's and we can demonstrate that the way he blew up your car matches the way he blew up cars in Northern Ireland we could be there.

'And I doubt Peddar's the type who's going to take the rap for the lot. He must be getting on now, he could go inside for most of the rest of his life. He'll not want to think Romano's out there still swanning about. Not if you drop the hint that he could do himself a bit of good fingering Romano.'

Jones's look of ingrained scepticism was beginning to change almost to elation. 'Do you think Helen might be persuaded to testify? About Romano's obsession to own The Fields and trying to persuade her that Todd's death had been drugs-related.'

'I think she might, you know. She's had her entire life pissed about by two evil, charming swine and she's one very angry lady.'

'We could organize witness protection.'

'She's a wealthy woman. She could lose herself abroad somewhere till the heat's off. You'll have another drink?'

Crane went to the bar. What a bleak affair it had all been: glamour, gambling, two cars demolished with the wrong men inside, a man who'd died twice. Apart from Milly, no one had come out of it very well, it had shades of the old black-and-white *films noirs*. The ramifications had seemed so endlessly complicated, including the tragedy of Milly's sister Sophie—

He went quickly back to the table. 'A separate matter, Terry, but still connected. That business at Hawksworth, a young woman drugged and dead in a Jacuzzi.'

Jones gave him a quizzical look. 'I remember it well. Too well. We got nowhere.'

'Well, Sophie Brown's sister was Milly, my friend at the casino.'

He told Jones what Milly had told him about Todd's association with Sophie and what Gerry Bishop had overheard

Todd planning in the interview room. 'I guess that was what Gerry was aiming to tell me the night he died. In case it had anything to do with Todd being killed.'

Crane spoke carefully. As far as he was concerned Todd really had died on the night his car was torched. He was prepared to gamble on the police never tying the body in the multistorey to Todd himself.

'I think you could use this information to lean on Morgan Walker,' Crane went on. 'He has no direct involvement but he's perverted the course of justice. He'll know damn well who Todd's mates were, if he was one himself. I reckon he's lived with a very guilty conscience since Sophie drowned. I doubt it would take much to make him crack. Probably glad to get it off his chest.'

Jones was beginning to look positively chirpy. 'It gets better and better. Do you think your little friend would testify?'

'Try and stop her. She and Sophie were closer than twins. All right, Todd was the ringleader and he's dead, but she wants to see the others punished.'

'We could have *two* results here, Frank. Well done, bloody well done.'

He'd made Jones's day. There was a faint wryness in Crane's smile, as any credit for the possible results would be down to Jones himself; that was how it worked in the force.

'Christ, Frank,' Jones said, grasping his arm, 'I wish you were back.'

Crane's smile became more open. He'd heard those words

from his old boss once or twice before. They never failed to make him feel good. They were really the only reward he needed from a man he respected as he did Terry Jones.